## "Twins?"

Becca's voice cracked. "I'd just gotten used to the idea of one child. And now there are two babies. The rules keep changing on me here. Or should I say the reality keeps changing. And multiplying."

Nick smiled at her. The smile reached his eyes, making them crinkle at the edges. Ooh, those incredible hypnotizing brown eyes that looked darker and more soulful than ever right now.

"Obviously I'm no expert, but I hear change is par for the course with children. Just when you think you have it all figured out, everything changes."

He shrugged.

"For someone who claims to know nothing about children, you sound pretty wise. But are you sure you're ready to do this?"

What a dumb question. They didn't really have any choice now. Or at least she didn't. She was still bracing herself, preparing for the moment that he changed his mind. And if learning that there was not one but two babies didn't send him running... She couldn't quite let down her guard and let herself go there yet.

* * *

**CELEBRATIONS, INC.: Let's get this party started!**

Dear Reader,

As I wrote *His Texas Christmas Bride*, I thought a lot about holiday traditions—the ones that have been passed down through the generations of my family and the ones that my husband and I have created with our daughter.

When our daughter was two, my husband and I had been so busy that we couldn't get our tree until Christmas week. The night we went to get it, all the pretty trees were gone. I think we hit every tree lot in central Florida, but we ended up with a little tree that even Charlie Brown might've rejected. From then on, we've gotten our tree the Saturday after Thanksgiving. It's become a tradition.

I borrowed that tradition for Becca Flannigan, the heroine of *His Texas Christmas Bride*. Becca loves traditions, especially during the holidays. Dr. Nick Ciotti, however, doesn't have time for such nonsense. Until the workaholic doctor meets warm, optimistic Becca and he realizes what he's been missing.

I hope you love Nick and Becca's story as much as I loved writing it. I also love hearing from readers. Please look me up on Facebook at facebook.com/nancyrobardsthompsonbooks, on Twitter, @NRTWrites, or drop me a line at nrobardsthompson@yahoo.com.

Happy holidays to you and yours!

*Nancy*

# His
# Texas Christmas
# Bride

———

## Nancy Robards Thompson

⟨H⟩ **HARLEQUIN**®SPECIAL EDITION®

Recycling programs
for this product may
not exist in your area.

ISBN-13: 978-0-373-65922-7

His Texas Christmas Bride

Copyright © 2015 by Nancy Robards Thompson

This edition published by arrangement with Harlequin Books S.A.

For questions and comments about the quality of this book, please contact us at CustomerService@Harlequin.com.

**Printed in U.S.A.**

www.Harlequin.com

National bestselling author **Nancy Robards Thompson** holds a degree in journalism. She worked as a newspaper reporter until she realized reporting "just the facts" bored her silly. Much more content to report to her muse, Nancy loves writing women's fiction and romance full-time. Critics have deemed her work "funny, smart and observant." She resides in Florida with her husband and daughter. You can reach her at nancyrobardsthompson.com and facebook.com/nancyrobardsthompsonbooks.

### Books by Nancy Robards Thompson

### Harlequin Special Edition

### *Celebrations, Inc.*

*How to Marry a Doctor*
*A Celebration Christmas*
*Celebration's Baby*
*Celebration's Family*
*Celebration's Bride*
*Texas Christmas*
*Texas Magic*
*Texas Wedding*

### *The Fortunes of Texas: Cowboy Country*

*My Fair Fortune*

### *The Fortunes of Texas:*
### *Welcome to Horseback Hollow*

*Falling for Fortune*

### *The Fortunes of Texas: Whirlwind Romance*

*Fortune's Unexpected Groom*

### *The Baby Chase*

*The Family They Chose*

*Accidental Heiress*
*Accidental Father*
*Accidental Cinderella*
*Accidental Princess*

Visit the Author Profile page at Harlequin.com for more titles.

This book is dedicated to Cindy Rutledge and Renee Halverson. You make writing so much fun!

## Chapter One

Becca Flannigan wasn't a gambler. For as far back as she could remember, she usually leaned toward the tried and true. She'd choose dependable, low-risk options over games of chance any day.

That's why it was particularly baffling when she discovered peace and the meaning of unconditional love with the simple flip of a coin.

Figuratively, of course. But she'd heard it said when you're uncertain about something, you should flip a coin. Even before the result turns up, you'll know what you want.

It was true.

The trip to Celebration Memorial Hospital's emergency room had been Becca Flannigan's bright, shiny quarter spinning in the air.

As she lay on the emergency room bed, one hand curled into the sheet and the other splayed protectively over her belly, she knew exactly what she wanted: she wanted—no, she *needed*—her unborn baby to be safe and healthy and unharmed by the bout of food poisoning that had landed her here in the hospital.

So, *this* was unconditional love, Becca thought as she tried to make sense of the foreign emotions that had commandeered her heart.

She'd never known a conviction like the one that had rooted itself deep in her soul; a certainty that she would die for the little being growing inside of her. But in this case, she couldn't die, because now there was something so much more important than herself to live for.

A few hours ago, the stabbing pain from the food poisoning had been so bad that death might have seemed preferable. But the terrifying realization that being this sick might cause her to lose the baby transcended the discomfort and became all consuming.

At barely three months pregnant, she hadn't been sure how she felt about her *situation*. Single and alone, she'd called it a predicament, a dilemma, a mess, a pickle—a gamble she'd taken and lost. She'd called it all those things, but she hadn't called it love until she'd faced the very real possibility of losing her child.

Here, under the harsh lights of the ER, something had cracked open inside her, and her previously muddied feelings had spilled away and everything important had crystallized.

Despite the fact that she didn't know how to find her child's father. She hadn't told her parents. Kate Thayer, her boss and best friend, was the only one who knew. The only reason Kate knew was because she'd been there with her in the ER when Becca had told the doctor.

Now the only thing that mattered was that the child growing inside her was safe and healthy.

This child was her everything.

At twelve weeks, she wasn't showing yet—although her body had started changing, a subtle transformation, adapting itself for the nine-month journey. She was thicker and her clothes fit snugly. People probably thought she'd gained weight. Just last week, her mother had made a snide comment about Becca spending too much time with Ben & Jerry's. Little did she know.

As Becca lay there with IV tubes in her arm and various machines beeping and humming, a restrained orchestration to accompany the chorus of emergency room sounds and voices on the other side of the cubicle curtain, she took back every negative or uncertain thought that had ever crossed her mind about this unplanned pregnancy.

She was single and only twenty-five years old. A baby hadn't been part of her plan at this juncture. They'd used protection that night. She wasn't supposed to take away a living, growing souvenir.

But now, faced with the possibility of losing her child, everything was suddenly different. If she lost this baby, this new capacity to love would surely die right along with it. Becca closed her eyes against the thought.

It wasn't going to happen. She wouldn't let it happen.

"How are you feeling, hon?" Becca opened her eyes to see Kate standing at the opening in the privacy curtain. Kate had driven Becca to the emergency room as soon as the nausea and pain had started.

The onset had hit Becca like an iron fist. One moment she was fine, walking from her desk to Kate's office with the mail, just as she did every single day, and the next thing she knew, she was doubled over in pain. Sensing something, or maybe Kate had heard Becca whimper, Kate had insisted on taking her to the hospital. "I got you some ice chips," Kate said. "I tried for water, but this was the best I could do. The nurse said she wants to make sure you can handle ice before she lets you have the hard stuff. They're pretty busy out there, and they're getting ready for a staff change. She said she'll try to pop in before she clocks out, but if she can't, she said the doctor who's coming on duty will be in to see you."

Becca did her best to smile as she accepted the white foam cup from Kate's outstretched hand. She felt like a wrung-out dishrag, but she was stable and the baby was okay.

Now she just wanted to go home.

"Thank you," Becca said, trying to steady her thin, shaky voice.

"I'd feed them to you, but—" Kate crinkled her nose as she held up her hands, motioning around with one "—it's a hospital and I haven't washed my hands. Plus, you'd probably bite me if I tried."

She smiled her sweet Kate smile. Becca did her best to smile back.

"Feeding me would be going above and beyond. I can handle it, thank you."

As Kate sat down, Becca lifted a piece of ice to her mouth, letting it linger on her parched lips. It melted on contact, leaving behind a cool, clean moisture. As she licked the droplets of water, Becca thought it was possibly the freshest, most delicious thing she'd ever tasted in her life. She placed another chip on her tongue. Surely this was what they meant when they'd said *nectar of the gods*.

Whoever *they* were. The ones who imparted such great wisdom about flipping coins and drinks fit for deities.

"How's the ice settling?" Kate asked.

Becca turned her head toward her friend, who had seated herself on a chair in the tiny space.

"I can't recall ever tasting anything so good," Becca said. "I highly recommend it."

She smiled at Kate, but Kate's smile didn't reach her worried eyes. "I'm glad you and the baby are going to be okay."

She knew her friend's words were sincere, but an unspoken question hung between them.

"No one else knows," Becca said. "About the baby, I mean. No one except you. And the doctor and nurses."

"You haven't told your family yet?"

Becca shook her head. She moved the cup of ice chips from her stomach to rest on the side of the bed. She needed to tell them. She probably should've already told them—before anyone else.

She'd wanted to be sure she'd make it through the first trimester...though, if she were being honest with herself, she hadn't really thought about telling them until now. But it made sense. No use in causing a family uproar for naught.

The thought made her shudder. She drew in a deep breath. Not only had her little one survived the first trimester, he or she had made it through this bout of food poisoning. This was a tenacious little being.

The words *meant to be* skipped through her head.

She would tell her parents.

Sometime soon…

As soon as she figured out how to explain.

They would ask about the father. That was the tricky part. What should she say? That his name was Nick and he was tall, gorgeous, and he'd swept her off her feet?

She'd met him at this very hospital the evening her nephew Victor had landed in this very emergency room that fateful evening three months earlier.

Nick. Nick who? Nick of the sultry brown eyes and the secret tattoos. Nick, who had been kind and generous in body and spirit and comfort. He'd been at the hospital that day interviewing for a job, which he hadn't taken or hadn't been offered. For whatever reason, he didn't work there now. Personnel wouldn't tell her why. They offered no help finding him. Of course, she hadn't told them she was pregnant. Not that it would've done any good. The woman with the horn-rimmed glasses had been so tight-lipped she might as well have been head of security at the Pentagon. She wasn't giving anything away. Oh, sure, she'd taken Becca's number and offered to pass it along. But Nick hadn't called.

Big surprise. They'd spent one night together. A night when her emotions had been raw. It was crazy because, judging by outward appearances—those tattoos, the motorcycle and that dark, penetrating gaze—he wasn't her type at all.

And what exactly was her type? It had been so long

since she'd been on a date that she couldn't really remember. Working at the Macintyre Foundation, she'd been so busy that she didn't have time for much of a social life. But that night with Nick, something intense and foreign had flared inside her. It hadn't mattered that he wasn't her type or that she didn't even really know the guy. She'd been inexplicably drawn to him, and in the midst of the rush, *type* hadn't even factored into the equation.

Of course, explaining this to her family would go over like a turd in the punch bowl. She was the good girl. She didn't do things like *that*. Especially not after her sister, Rosanna, had gotten pregnant in high school. Nope. Rosanna had been the bad example, the cautionary tale about why you didn't sleep with men who didn't love you.

Becca's hand found her stomach again. If she'd stayed at the hospital the night of Victor's accident, life would be drastically different right now.

"Do you want to talk about it?" Kate asked.

She shrugged. "I do, but not here."

"Of course." Kate sat forward on her chair. "There's no privacy here. And you're probably not up to it right now. But, Becs, I'm here for you. Okay?"

Kate reached out and squeezed Becca's hand.

"Whatever you need," she added.

Becca forced a smile. She recalled how her mother used to tell her it took more muscles to frown than it did to smile. At the moment, nothing could have felt further from the truth.

"Thank you, Kate. You've already done so much for me today."

And she had. Kate had spent the afternoon in the

emergency room with her. By now, Kate's family would be home. Her husband, Liam Thayer, was head of Celebration Memorial pediatrics. He was one of the bigwigs at the hospital. Becca had thought about asking him to do a little sleuthing on her behalf to help her locate Nick.

Now that Kate knew, maybe she would. She'd be asking Liam to break the rules. And of course, she'd have to offer a pretty darned good explanation as to why she wanted personal info about a doctor who had interviewed at the hospital three months ago. That would mean she'd have to admit to Liam she'd slept with a man without even knowing his last name.

Other than pride, she couldn't think of a good reason not to ask Liam to help her get an address or phone number, something more to go on than simply *Nick, the hot doctor from San Antonio.*

He was the father of her baby. He deserved to know.

But she and Kate would have that conversation another time. She couldn't chance someone who worked in the ER overhearing them plotting to infiltrate hospital human resources.

Right now, her throat and lips were too dry to talk, and she was utterly exhausted. It took all the energy she possessed to place another ice chip in her mouth and close her eyes.

She wasn't sure how long she'd been lying there drifting in and out of light sleep, dreams merging with the sounds in the ER; dreams of the night of Victor's accident when her sister had been crazed with worry and had taken it out on Becca. She dreamed of Rosanna screaming at her, telling her to get out.

Blaming her for what happened. And then the dream morphed into meeting Nick, making love to Nick…

That's why she wasn't sure if she was dreaming or if she really had sensed him standing there. But when she opened her eyes at the sound of someone pulling open the curtain surrounding her bed, Nick *was* standing there.

"Hi, Ms. Flannigan. I'm Dr. Ciotti." He was looking down at the tablet in his hands, not at her.

It was *him*. All tall six-foot-something of him. Slightly longish brown hair. The lab coat and green scrubs didn't hide the mile-wide shoulders, but they covered up the tattoos on his biceps.

God, those tattoos. One of them, a single word—Latin, she thought, but she wasn't sure. The other was an ornate Celtic cross, which she found fascinating—especially now, because based on his last name, Ciotti, Nick Ciotti—his background might be Italian.

She'd memorized those tattoos. Just as she'd memorized the feel of the long, lean muscled planes of that body. Despite her weakened state, recalling these details had her feeling the same brand of hot and bothered she'd felt *that night*, the night they'd first met.

And now he was standing in front of her. As if she'd conjured him.

Becca blinked. What was he doing here? When she'd tried to find him, the people in the human resources department had sworn there was not a doctor with the first name of Nick employed at Celebration Memorial.

Maybe he was some dark angel who'd been sentenced to serve purgatory in emergency rooms… Okay, she wasn't so out of it that she didn't realize how delusional that sounded. Or that she probably had never looked worse. Maybe he wouldn't recognize her.

*And that would be preferable?*

*Maybe.*

"I've just come on duty after a shift change, and I wanted to look in on you before signing your release papers."

Had she conjured him? Or maybe she was hallucinating?

"How are you feeling?" he asked as he keyed something into the tablet, still not looking up. "I understand you're pregnant. Are you feeling strong enough to go home?"

She didn't quite know what to say. Especially since her entire body had gone numb at the sight of him.

When he finally looked up, their gazes met. His upright professionalism gave way to recognition. Recognition morphed into something that resembled utter shock. But it took only a couple of beats for him to compose himself. Becca could see the virtual wall go up around him.

"Hello," he said. "It's, uh—it's nice to see you again."

His words were clipped and matter-of-fact. There was no trace of the sex god who had zapped her of all common sense and discretion *that night*.

"It's been a while, hasn't it?" She tried to keep her voice light. It wasn't an easy task, lying there on a gurney in a hospital gown, with parched lips and a dry mouth. How many times had she imagined running into him at a park or in a restaurant—in her imagination he was always dining solo, of course, waiting for her and overjoyed by the reunion. But the one scenario she'd never imagined was running into him as a patient in the emergency room, looking as she felt right now.

*God, just kill me now.*

She instantly regretted the figurative words. Her hand automatically moved to her belly in a protective stance.

She took a deep breath and reframed. This wasn't the time for vanity. So what if her hair was a mess and her makeup had washed away hours ago? No matter what she looked like right now, she had important matters to discuss with him.

"How long has it been?" he asked. His shock and surprise had settled into a professional half smile that put miles of space between them. The expression established that they were acquaintances. That he was the doctor and she was the patient, and doctors didn't sleep with their patients.

But until now, she hadn't been his patient. He had only helped her out by answering questions about her nephew's condition. Medical terms she hadn't understood and he'd explained to her.

"It's been three months," Becca offered. "Twelve weeks, almost exactly to the date."

Dr. Nick *Ciotti* glanced down again at the tablet in his hands. He scrolled with his fingertip. "Yes. So, it's been…three months."

She could see him doing the math in his head.

Nick turned to the nurse, whom Becca had just noticed, and Kate. "Would you give me a moment with Ms. Flannigan, please?"

*Ms. Flannigan?* What?

As if she didn't feel unattractive enough, now he was making her feel like the mean woman who ran the orphanage in *Annie*. Wait, no, that was Miss Hannigan. Still, no one called her Ms. Flannigan. Especially not the hot guy who'd gotten her pregnant.

The nurse cast him a look.

"It will be fine, Sally. Becca and I are old friends. We need to catch up."

*Old friends?* She forced herself to not look at Kate. If she looked at Kate, she was sure Sally would be able to see everything in the glance they'd exchange.

Nick met Becca's eyes again. "I'm sure your friend won't mind giving us a moment, will she?"

Becca opened her mouth to answer. However, suddenly, she didn't want Kate to leave.

But she and Nick needed to talk. The thought of being alone with him knocked the wind out of her.

"Becca?" Kate asked. "Is that okay?"

What was she supposed to say? *No? Don't leave me?*

God, she was so unprepared for this. Then again, it seemed as if she'd been unprepared for everything these past three months.

Just another day in her life. Only this one included the father of her child. The thought sent her freefalling.

She nodded. "It's fine."

Sally looked dubious, but she motioned for Kate to follow her. "Are you sure you're okay?" Kate asked.

"I'm fine," Becca repeated.

"We shouldn't be long," Nick said, his gaze trained on the tablet in his hands.

Kate cast an uncertain glance at Nick, but she followed Sally out into the emergency room. Once they'd cleared the curtain, an awkward silence stretched between Nick and Becca.

Nick lowered his voice. "It's good to see you again."

"Quite a surprise," she said. "I didn't realize you'd taken the job."

"I didn't at first," he said. "But we finally came to a meeting of the minds. So, is there something we need to talk about?"

"Yes, we have quite a bit to talk about," Becca said. As Nick watched her lips move, he tried to process what was happening.

Becca Flannigan looked like the girl next door with her silky brown hair and piercing blue eyes with golden flecks and a navy circle around the iris. They were the kind of eyes that tempted a guy to stare a little too long. That's what had happened the night he'd met her, when her sister had been screaming at her, telling her to leave the hospital, blaming Becca for her son's accident, even though the kid had admitted he'd been drag racing. As he was on his way out after interviewing for the ER job, he'd witnessed Becca trying to ask a question about her nephew's condition, and then he'd watched the boy's mother tear into her. He probably shouldn't have—he should've left well enough alone and gone back to his hotel—but as Becca had been walking away, he'd called her back and answered her question.

She'd looked so fragile that night, some protective instinct had sprung to life. He'd wanted to help her, set her mind at ease.

Even now she stirred that same visceral reaction that had previously attracted Nick. And when he'd walked into Bentleys across from the hospital to get some dinner before going back to his hotel and saw her sitting there, she'd been a ray of sunshine on his gray horizon of plans.

And he realized Becca had been talking, but he hadn't heard a single word she'd said—except for *pregnant* and *yes, we absolutely need to talk.*

In the span of five minutes his entire world had upended. He couldn't be a father. Well, yeah, he could be, but they'd used a condom. How had this happened?

He raked a hand through his hair as unsavory words galloped through his mind. What if this wasn't his baby? What proof did he have other than one night with her around the time of conception? How well did he know this woman? He didn't, beyond the fact that he'd been mesmerized by her that lone night three months ago.

He set his jaw to ensure his thoughts didn't become words and escape into the ether.

Instead, he said, "Would you like to tell me how this happened?"

Becca frowned at him as if he was an idiot, and he realized how that must've sounded. *Idiotic.*

"Never mind," he amended. "I'm—"

Something clattered on the other side of the curtains—a dropped supply tray, maybe, or something else metallic and noisy. Somewhere in the distance, a child cried, "I want my mommy." He could hear one of the nurses in the adjacent area conversing with a patient as if she were standing next to him talking in his ear.

Suddenly, everything seemed amplified. They couldn't talk about this here. Nick trained his eyes on the patient chart tablet for a long moment, trying to gather his thoughts—looking for something, anything, that might right this rapidly sinking ship. Her emergency contact was her friend Kate, or at least he assumed it was Kate. Kate Thayer, the chart read, friend. No husband or boyfriend or significant other. Becca had named her parents as next of kin. Which completely eliminated the possibility that she'd gotten married since the last time—the only time—he'd seen her. But wait—he scrolled back up to the top of her chart to check. Yes, marital status was listed as single.

He looked back at Becca.

She was the last person he'd dreamed he'd run into today.

He'd wanted to see her again. In fact, he'd thought about her often since that night. When he'd finally accepted the job, he'd planned on trying to look her up. How many Beccas could there be in Celebration, Texas? But he hadn't had much spare time lately. Between wrapping up his job in San Antonio and moving to Celebration, he'd been slammed. He'd been in town only five days. His possessions were still in boxes stacked inside his apartment because he'd hit the ground running since moving.

And here they were. Reunited.

And she was three months pregnant. He didn't need a calculator to do that math.

"When did you get back into town?" she asked.

Her question answered something that had been lurking in the back of his mind. Had she come here looking for him?

Of course she hadn't. It said right on her chart

that food poisoning had brought her into the emergency room.

Then another question elbowed its way into the forefront of his mind: When had she planned on telling him? Was it even part of her plan? If he hadn't changed his mind and accepted the job, would he have even known about the pregnancy?

"I've been here less than a week."

"I see." He glimpsed a note of sadness in her eyes. Or maybe she was simply mirroring his own confusion back at him.

She looked small and fragile lying there. Despite everything—the bombshell, the uncertainty—he still had the damnedest urge to gather her in his arms and protect her.

Wasn't that how they'd gotten into this situation in the first place?

With that thought firmly in mind, he reminded himself that he was at work. In this moment he was her attending physician. Thoughts like that were off-limits. She was off-limits.

"Sally will be here in a moment to check your vitals. When everything checks out, you can go home. You'll want to follow up with your obstetrician, and, of course, if you start feeling ill, call your doctor. Or come back to the emergency room. If it's an emergency."

She was quiet while he updated her chart.

When he'd finished, essentially signing off as her doctor, he said, "When are you available?"

"Excuse me?"

"We need to talk."

She shrugged, then lowered her voice. "Listen,

I'm not going to try to force you into anything you don't want to do."

"Let's not talk about this here."

Even though he hadn't meant to offend her, and he wasn't putting her off—he was on the clock, and they needed privacy—she looked offended.

"When are you available?" he repeated.

"I don't know. I guess, whenever I feel stronger."

Really, there was no sense in delaying.

"How about tomorrow?" he said.

## *Chapter Two*

Thirty minutes later, Becca was in Kate's car on her way home. It was cold outside on this mid-November evening and she felt the chill down to her bones. It amplified how weak and vulnerable she felt.

Despite how she'd wanted to reconnect with Nick, how she'd tried to find him right after she'd found out that she was pregnant, she hadn't been prepared for the reunion to happen this way.

Even though he deserved to know the truth, she'd wanted the disclosure to be on her terms. The vulnerable side of her wished she was still safe in her cocoon, the only one who knew about the baby. No one to please. No one to convince that this child was wanted and dear and loved—even if he or she was a surprise. She had just come to terms with the situation herself. Now things had suddenly gotten complicated again.

Becca stared out the passenger-side window into the inky sky. The trees were beginning to shed their leaves and stood stark and bare in the chill night.

How symbolic, she thought. Exposed. Stripped down to the naked branches with nothing to hide what lay beneath. Somewhere from deep inside, a voice reminded her that some of these trees had lined Celebration's Main Street for centuries. They'd endured winters and storms and climate changes to see another season.

This was simply a new season of her life.

Nick was coming over tomorrow to talk. While she understood that he needed time to digest the news— just as she had—he hadn't seemed very happy about it. And she wasn't sure she was ready to deal with that right now. But if not now, when?

When they stopped at a red light, Becca felt Kate's gaze on her. Kate was such a good friend. This was all fresh news to her—huge news that her best friend was pregnant and going it alone. Well, not exactly alone. Not anymore. So, it was actually a double bit of juiciness, and not once since they'd left the hospital had Kate pushed her to give up the goods.

Becca knew she didn't owe anyone an explanation, but Kate did deserve to know what was going on.

"So, I'm pregnant," Becca offered. "And Nick is the father."

Kate's eyes were wide, but all she did was nod.

"I probably should've told you sooner so that you didn't find out like this, but I wasn't ready to tell anyone. Still, I hope you know how much I appreciate all you've done today. You're such a good friend, Kate."

"I'm glad I was here for you today," she said. "For

the record, you don't have to tell anyone anything until you're ready."

The two sat in silence and Becca let the solidarity wash over her.

"But he is a good-looking guy," Kate added. "I can see the temptation."

A hiccup of a laugh escaped Becca, and for a moment the tension lifted. "I know, right?"

Kate's curiosity was almost palpable.

"Liam's never mentioned Dr. Ciotti."

The statement was a question. Kate was testing the water to see how Becca would warm to telling her more. The light turned green, and Kate accelerated at a gentle pace.

"He hasn't even been at the hospital a week," Becca said. "Since they're in different departments, I'm not surprised he hasn't mentioned him. They may not have met yet."

That was a long shot. The hospital wasn't large. Most of the staff knew each other at least by sight.

"How did you two meet?" Kate ventured. "You don't have to answer that if you're not ready to talk about it."

The cat was already out of the bag. She couldn't blame Kate for being curious. If the situation were reversed, she'd want to know. Then again, Kate was married to a fabulous man. It was a relationship made in heaven, though it hadn't started out that way. Her husband, Liam, had been a widower when Kate had first met him. He came with adorable twin teenage girls and the expected amount of baggage that a man who had lost his first love much too young would bring to a new relationship. But Liam and Kate were soul mates. Despite fate's cruel curveball, they'd been given a chance at happiness, and they'd taken it.

Becca tried to keep her mind from wandering to the possibility that she and Nick might be soul mates.

She really shouldn't go there. For her own peace of mind.

The best way to make sure she didn't was to tell Kate the story of the night she met Nick.

"No, it's okay. I don't mind. Remember the night that Victor got in the drag racing accident?"

"Yes."

"That night at the hospital Rosanna was so mad at me."

Kate slanted her a glance. "Why was she mad at you? You weren't driving."

"I wasn't, but I was the one who taught Victor how to drive a standard transmission."

They came to a stop sign, and Kate shot her a glance that conveyed she clearly didn't understand Rosanna's anger.

Really, who did understand her sister? It seemed as if she was angry most of the time.

"She said if I hadn't taught him, he wouldn't have been tempted." Becca shrugged. "That's Rosanna logic for you. But I know she was just upset. Victor was banged up pretty badly. Anyhow, when the doctor came to give us the prognosis, I asked him to clarify something, and Rosanna tore into me. She told me I didn't get to ask questions. She told me to leave.

"I wanted to give her some space, so I walked away. I went over to the nurses' station to get a cup of coffee. I just wanted to give her a chance to calm down. When I was pouring the coffee, this guy—this drop-dead-gorgeous guy—was standing there, and he told me he didn't mean to butt in, but he couldn't help but overhear the exchange with my sister. Everybody had heard her, I'm sure. He told me he was a doctor, and he explained what Victor's doctor had said."

"That was Nick?" Kate asked.

Becca nodded.

"And then what? Did he ask for your phone number?"

Becca ran a hand over her eyes. *Ugh.* This was so embarrassing. Kate knew her well enough to know she didn't sleep around. In fact, the last time she'd had sex was with her boyfriend two years ago.

"Not exactly. I went back over and rejoined my family, but Rosanna was just hysterical. My dad suggested that it might be a good idea to give her some space. He told me to go get something to eat, which really meant I should disappear for a while. He said he'd call if there were any changes in Victor's condition.

"So, I walked over to Bentleys across the street from the hospital. I was just going to sit there for a while, get a decent cup of coffee—the stuff at the nurses' station tasted like dirty water, and it was only lukewarm. I was going to bring some coffee back for my folks and Rosanna. A peace offering. I just wanted to give her a little time.

"And who do you suppose walked into Bentleys?"

"Nick?"

"How did you guess?" Becca laughed, but the sound was dry and brittle. It wasn't funny. It was embarrassing. Kind of pathetic, really.

"That night Nick and I seemed to be on a trajectory toward each other. I came in and sat down at a booth and ordered my coffee. And for some reason everything that had been bottled up began spilling out. I started crying, and I couldn't stop. I mean, I wasn't making a scene or anything, but the tears just wouldn't stop. The next thing I knew, I saw Nick through the window. He was parking a motorcycle, and a minute later, he was standing by my table, offering me a napkin for my tears."

"And the rest is history?"

"After he'd told me what the doctor had said, he'd checked on Victor and learned that, though he was banged up pretty badly, he was stable. He was going to be fine. And then the rest is history."

Even though they were both adults, and she knew Kate wouldn't think badly of her, Becca couldn't look at her friend. Instead, she stared straight ahead.

"I've never had a one-night stand before," Becca said. "I do, and look what happens."

They were in front of Becca's condo now. Kate killed the engine and reached out and put a hand on Becca's arm. "Honey, I'm not judging you. You're a grown woman, and you're free to do whatever you want with your body. As long as you're *safe*—"

"We used protection." She hadn't meant to sound so defensive. She took a deep breath and tempered her tone. "Obviously, something went wrong."

Kate nodded. "What are you going to do now?"

Becca shrank into the shadows as she watched two of her neighbors, Mrs. Milton and Mrs. Cavett, who had the condos on either side of her, extract themselves from Mrs. Milton's ancient Cadillac Deville. Mrs. M's late husband had purchased the car brand-new, and she was still so proud of it she'd tell anyone who'd care to listen. If Becca had heard the story once, she'd heard it twenty-five times.

For that matter, both of her neighbors loved to gossip. People affectionately called them the Busybody Twins. Between the two of them, they prided themselves on knowing everything about everyone who lived in the sixty units at Lake Celebration Landing Condos. What they didn't know, they made up.

Once they learned of Becca's pregnancy, word would be all over the tiny condo complex.

Becca shouldn't care. She shouldn't let other people's opinions of her matter. But it did matter. She'd always been the good girl, the one people could count on, the community-minded good example.

Now she'd be known as the one who got knocked up.

*Well, it is what it is.*

She just needed to make sure her baby didn't grow up feeling like a mistake.

"I'm going to have a baby," she said. "Tomorrow, Nick is coming over, and we're going to figure it out."

Nick steered his motorcycle into a parking space at the Lake Celebration Landing Condominiums, a neatly landscaped, compact grouping of townhomes on the east side of Celebration.

His gaze picked out unit four. Becca's place. Glossy ceramic planters with yellow and rust-colored flowers flanked the red front door, which sported a wreath of wheat stalks and small pumpkins—or were those gourds? It was hard to tell. Whatever they were, they screamed fall and hinted that Becca took a lot of pride in her home.

The amber porch light glowed in the dusk. She was waiting for him. Or she was home, at least. Of course she was; she was expecting him, even if last night as he'd signed her discharge papers she hadn't seemed overly eager to see him. He swung his leg over the bike's seat and stood, hesitating a moment.

Was a person ever really ready for a conversation like this? Yesterday morning when he'd opened his eyes, he'd had no idea how his life was about to change.

But they had a lot to talk about. He'd made a list. Because he knew if he didn't write down the important things he might get distracted. Becca Flannigan made him stupid like that.

Nick hated acting stupid. Stupid equaled out of control, and out of control usually ended in disaster.

He reached in the storage console on his bike and pulled out a paper grocery bag. It contained chicken noodle soup and a small box of saltines. Becca was probably sick of bland food by now. But at least it was something. He wasn't showing up empty-handed, he thought as he knocked on the door above the wreath.

He heard a dog bark and then a soft murmuring he imagined was her way of gently quieting the animal.

Funny, he knew so little about this woman. As he stood on her front porch, it almost felt like a blind date. However, when she answered his knock, and he saw her there, looking much more like herself, or at least more like the woman who had swept him away when they'd met, he felt that attraction, that visceral pull that had hit him hard that first night.

She wore blue jeans and a simple blue blouse that brought out the color of her eyes. She'd pulled her golden-brown hair away from her face with a black headband. She didn't wear much makeup. The color had returned to her cheeks, and her skin looked so smooth he had to fight the urge to reach out and touch her.

"Hi," he said.

"Hi, Nick." The dog, a red-and-white, low-to-the-ground model, barked a greeting and jumped up on his leg.

"Hey, there, buddy," Nick said.

"Priscilla, get down. I'm sorry about that. Just tell her no, and she'll stand down."

"It's okay." He dropped to one knee, setting the bag down so he could use both hands to scratch the dog behind her ears. The animal showed her appreciation by jumping up again and licking Nick's nose.

"Priscilla. Stop it," Becca said. "Mind your manners."

"She's a corgi?" Nick asked as he got to his feet.

"Yes. A very spoiled corgi who needs to learn how to listen."

Nick smiled. "We had a corgi when I was growing up. They're great dogs."

"Yes, they are. Come in."

She stepped back to allow him room to pass. As he stepped into the foyer, he could smell the faint scent of her perfume—something floral—which brought him back to that night. As it had before, it tempted him to lean in closer and breathe in the essence of her. His mind flashed back to how she'd looked as he'd made love to her—soft and sweet and incredibly sexy in an understated way that had driven him mad.

He blinked away the thought and held out the bag.

"What's this?" she asked.

"It's for you. Although you probably don't need it now. You look like you're feeling better."

He'd been at the hospital from 7:00 p.m. to 7:00 a.m. And then he'd gone home to get some sleep. When he'd called her this afternoon to confirm she was up for meeting this evening, she'd said she was fine. She'd taken the day off from work to rest. Since they were meeting tonight, it hadn't made sense to drop it by earlier. Besides, it might've given her the wrong idea. That he wanted more than he was prepared to give.

It was all true and valid.

So, why did he feel like a jerk?

"Thanks." She accepted the grocery bag and peered into it. "Ah, soup and crackers. Thank you. I'm almost completely back to normal, except for being a little tired. But that's par for the course lately."

She shrugged and ducked her head as she turned away to shut the door. Her body language made her seem a little vulnerable in the wake of her admission.

Nick had taken a few steps out of the small foyer and into the nicely decorated living room before she caught up with him. The room, which featured shades of greens and blues, had a traditional feel, but it certainly wasn't old stodgy traditional. It looked as if she'd put a lot of thought into the decor. Still, it wasn't so decorated that he couldn't imagine kicking back and watching the Cowboys or the Mavericks on a flat-screen on a lazy Sunday afternoon.

His mind tried to lead him to other things they could do on a lazy afternoon, but he reminded himself why he was here tonight, and the thought was instantly sobering.

"Sit down." She gestured toward a couple of chairs

arranged across from the couch that were upholstered in a blue-and-green geometric pattern. The couch—a big, overstuffed number—looked a hell of a lot more comfortable, but tonight wasn't about comfort. It was about figuring things out.

He took a seat on the closest chair.

The dog had trotted into the room with a rawhide in her mouth and plopped down next to his feet, ready to do some damage to her chew toy.

"May I get you something to drink?" she asked.

He wondered if she meant wine or beer or something tamer like water or coffee. The only thing they'd had the night they met was coffee. He didn't even know if she drank.

His gaze drifted over her stomach for a quick moment. Of course she wouldn't imbibe alcohol now.

"I'm good," he said. "But thanks."

She sat on the couch across from him.

"You worked today?" she asked.

So, they were going to make small talk before they got to the heart of the matter. Okay, for a few minutes. His ex-wife had told him he wasn't good at chitchat. According to her, he wasn't good at communicating. Period.

It was true; he usually didn't have the patience for meaningless conversation. What was the point? That's why he didn't care for cocktail and dinner parties, and it was a big part of the reason he was divorced now.

That and his tendency to be a workaholic. Delilah had complained a lot about him never being home. He'd told her that was life with an ER doctor. Eventually, she'd left him for his best friend, who also happened to own the lawn service that did their yard.

He wasn't sure which was sadder…the fact that their breakup had been such a cliché—the only thing that could've been worse was if she'd left him for the pool boy—or the overwhelming sense of relief he'd felt after he'd signed the divorce papers.

After that, he'd buried himself in work. Emergency medicine suited him so well. It was fast-paced and involved a revolving door of patients. He could keep it all about work and not get too personal. He'd make sure they were stable and hand them off to their primary care doctor.

It was clean and simple. No need for small talk or building relationships beyond the situation that had brought them into his emergency room.

"I've worked twelve-hour shifts for the past five days. Actually, it's my first night off since I took the job."

"Are they ganging up on the new guy?" She smiled and her dimples winked at him.

"No, they've been so shorthanded that the other doctors haven't had much time off in a while."

She was quiet for a moment and he could see the wheels turning in her mind. She glanced at her hands, which were in her lap, before looking back at him.

"Why didn't you take the job at first?" she asked. "Because they did offer it to you, didn't they? Please, tell me you didn't decline because of what happened between us."

A pretty shade of pink bloomed on her cheeks.

"Wait, don't answer that," she said. "It's a dumb question. Of course you didn't turn down a job because of me. It's just that I tried to get in touch with you after I found out I was pregnant, but all the hospital would tell me was that you didn't work there."

He nodded. So she'd tried to find him. He wondered if she'd been discreet when she was doing her detective work. No one had told him that a woman claiming to be carrying his child had been there looking for him. Then again, how would an employer break that news to a new hire? And would she really have told a complete stranger *why* she was looking for him? Not likely.

"I couldn't justify relocating on the first offer," he said. "But I could work with their counteroffer. So, just in case you were still wondering, no, my turning it down had nothing to do with you or what happened between us."

"I didn't even know your last name," she said.

Exactly. They hadn't exchanged much personal information beyond first names. He'd thought that was the way she'd wanted it, and it had made their meeting sexy and exciting.

"So, I take it you're keeping the baby."

"Of course I am. I have a good job. This place isn't a palace, but it's big enough for a child and me."

They sat in silence for a moment. The furnace ticked and then clicked on. A car honked somewhere outside.

"Look," she finally said, "I won't try to force you to be part of this child's life. We will be perfectly fine on our own. I just thought you should know."

"Would you be willing to take a paternity test?"

"Excuse me?"

"A paternity test. Would you take one?"

Her mouth opened and shut before she could utter a word.

It wasn't an unreasonable request, but the way she glared at him made it seem as if he'd asked her to move to Mars. The look in her eyes cut him deeply.

But he couldn't go there. Or rather, he couldn't let her work her way into that soft spot where instinct and feelings lived and eclipsed common sense. Instinct and feelings had never served him well. That's how they'd gotten themselves into this mess in the first place. He made a mental note not to call the pregnancy—or the baby—a mess. If she was reacting this way to a paternity test, she'd probably smack him if he called the situation a mess.

It was all so new that the pregnancy and baby didn't seem as if they were one and the same. That *his* child might be growing inside Becca...

The thought hit him like a punch in the gut. He would not make a good father. He was married to his job. Children were too unpredictable. They were too fragile. He knew for a fact he did not do well with unpredictable and fragile. He'd learned the hard way. The ER was a different type of unpredictable. It was based in science and methodical procedure. He never knew what he'd get one night to the next in the ER, but no matter what was thrown at him, he could follow procedure and tame the chaos. He could fix people.

But being a father? Raising a child? God help him. Or more accurate, God help the poor child.

That's as far as he could go right now.

He simply couldn't wrap his mind around it. But

there was no sense in getting shell-shocked until he had the facts in hand.

He knew he sounded like a first-class jerk, but the sad truth was he wouldn't be able to wrap his mind around the pregnancy until he was certain the baby was his.

Yes, she was three months pregnant. Yes, he'd slept with her twelve weeks ago. But they'd been together one night. He didn't know her or how many guys she'd slept with or when she'd slept with them. Even though he didn't want to believe she'd try to saddle him with another man's kid.

But he didn't really know her. Because of this, he reminded himself, it wasn't out of line to ask for proof that he was the father.

"We used a condom," he said. "I just don't see how this could've happened."

She squinted at him and did a little head jut.

"Hello, you're a doctor. You, of all people, should know that condoms aren't one hundred percent fail-safe."

He shrugged. "You're right. They aren't foolproof. But they do prevent pregnancy most of the time. I need a paternity test for my own peace of mind. It's not you, it's me. When you get the test and the results come back, you can tell me I'm a jackass and say *I told you so* as many times as you want."

She scoffed and shook her head, obviously disgusted with him.

"Becca, don't be mad, please."

"I'm not mad at you. Because even though I don't sleep around, Nick—before you, I'd never had a one-night stand, and after I got the news, I wished I never had—you couldn't possibly know me well enough to know that. So I'm not mad at you. I'm mad at myself for sleeping with a man who doesn't know me well enough to know that."

## Chapter Three

Just as Nick had maintained that he was within his right to ask Becca to take the paternity test, she was justified in feeling offended and irritated by his request.

However, the all-too-rational part of Becca's brain knew without a doubt how the results would come back. It would prove that Nick was the father. So, why argue?

*Why?*

Insult and exasperation kicked up again. *Do the words* it's the principle of the matter *not mean anything to you?*

Her heart had broken a little bit after Nick's visit. Still tender, it tried to overrule that sickeningly reasonable voice in her brain.

She didn't *have to* take the test if she didn't want to. He wasn't strong-arming her. She didn't need to prove herself. But wouldn't it look as if she had something to hide if she held out? The truth would set her free.

Or would it?

Handing Nick proof positive would not guarantee he'd be any happier about it than he was right now. But that was the chance she'd have to take. She'd meant it when she'd told him she wouldn't try to force him into anything he didn't want to do. And she wouldn't.

In the end, vindication trumped justification. The next day she went to the lab in Dallas that Nick had recommended and let them draw blood for a non-invasive prenatal paternity test. They told her they'd have the results back in two business days.

After the longest two days of her life, Becca braced herself for the news. She wasn't sure why she was anxious, since the results wouldn't be a surprise. But last night she'd dreamed that the lab had gotten her results mixed up with another person's, and she couldn't seem to make Nick understand that it was a mistake. That the lab had messed up.

All her life Becca, who'd been a straight-A student up through college, had had recurring nightmares of failing tests. They'd only served as incentive to work harder. But this test was out of her control.

As she took the parking garage elevator into the lobby of the Macintyre Enterprises building, she took a deep breath and tried to get in touch with her rational mind, which still seemed to be fast asleep this morning.

Her foolish, emotional, battered heart was not only wide-awake and beating like a cymbal-banging monkey, it had been making her do crazy things like check her email every fifteen minutes since five-thirty this morning. If her rational mind cared to show up, it would convince her that, much like pressing an elevator button repeatedly when waiting for a slow car, refreshing her email browser every fifteen minutes before the workaday world had poured their first cup of coffee was fruitless.

But sometimes exercises in futility were therapeutic.

She stepped off the garage elevator into the lobby and turned toward the bank of elevators that would carry her up to her office on the top floor of the building.

The Macintyre Foundation was housed in a twenty-five-story glass-and-chrome building in the heart of downtown Dallas. The Macintyre Family Foundation shared office space with Macintyre Enterprises, which belonged to Kate's brother, Rob Macintyre. The foundation mostly served the community of Celebration, Texas, which was located about twenty minutes outside of downtown Dallas. But since Rob Macintyre owned the Dallas-based building, they couldn't beat the cost of rent.

Every time Becca stepped into the massive glass-enclosed lobby, she looked up. She couldn't help herself, even after all these years. The ceiling seemed to stretch miles above her head, reaching toward the heavens. All around a gentle green-tinted light filtered in. Even in the soft morning sunshine, it reflected off the chrome furniture, fixtures and giant fountain in the center of the atrium.

Everything about the space was sleek and polished, and this morning it felt particularly cold and fed her anxious nerves, which just proved she needed a hot beverage to warm her up, because there wasn't anything cold about the Macintyre family. They did a lot of good for the Celebration community.

Becca tightened her cashmere scarf and turned up the collar on her red wool coat to stave off the chill that had worked its way into her bones. She'd worn her favorite gray tweed skirt and ivory cashmere sweater to bolster herself against the emotional day. The ensemble was soft and warm, a comfort outfit, if there was such a thing, even if it was fitting a little snug these days.

She took off her hat, smoothed her hair into place and waved good morning to Violet, the receptionist who tended the lobby concierge desk. Even though Violet was small, young and pretty and very feminine, she was the gatekeeper, and she took her job seriously. No one got past her unless they had an appointment or possessed a preapproved security badge. Nobody wanted to tangle with Violet.

The heels of Becca's boots tapped a cadence on the marble floors. The sound seemed to carry and echo in the cavernous lobby. Today, all of her senses were heightened. Even so, she tried to walk a little more carefully to muffle the noise.

When Becca finally reached the twenty-fifth floor, the office was quiet. Kate, Rob and his wife, Pepper, who was in charge of the foundation's community relations department, obviously hadn't gotten to work yet. Becca was so early even their receptionist, Lisa, wasn't there.

After Becca turned on the office lights, she made her way to the kitchenette, where she started a pot of coffee for the office and brewed herself a cup of herbal tea.

God, the coffee smelled good. It took every ounce of strength she possessed not to toss the tea—a spicy, fruity blend that Kate had brought in for Becca after she'd learned about the pregnancy and Becca's subsequent caffeine sacrifice.

Caffeine wasn't good for the baby. That was the only incentive she needed to fortify her willpower. She grabbed her caffeine-free infusion and headed straight to her office away from temptation. At least the insipid liquid was hot and had begun to take the edge off the chill she'd experienced as she drove into work.

Fall was one of Becca's favorite seasons. She loved everything about it, from the pumpkins and the autumn leaves as they shrugged off the last vestiges of summer green and donned glorious harvest colors, to the nip in the air and the way the community seemed to come together even more at football games and festivals. Becca had decorated her office to set a festive mood. A garland of leaves and straw artfully woven together festooned her office door, and she had brought in her pumpkin-spice-scented candle. Before she sat down at her desk, she turned on her electric candle warmer.

She had a long to-do list to plow through today, lots to accomplish to make sure Celebration's fourth annual Central Park tree-lighting ceremony, an event the foundation sponsored the day after Thanksgiving, went off perfectly. The event had become a beloved tradition for the Celebration community, and if Becca had it her way, she'd do her part to make it better and better every year.

But even that had to wait. Because the first thing she did after she booted up her computer was check her email to see if there was any word from the lab.

The tech had given her a password and told her that after she received the email alerting her that her test results were ready, she was to go to a website, enter the password and retrieve her exoneration.

He'd called it results, of course, not exoneration, but that's how she'd come to think of it.

Of course, since it wasn't even nine o'clock, the email hadn't yet arrived. She took a fortifying sip of tea and uttered a silent prayer that they wouldn't make her wait until the end of the day.

But wait—what if she'd miscalculated? Was today considered day two? Or was that tomorrow? The cymbal monkey kicked in again, and her heart virtually rattled at the thought. She didn't know if she could bear to wait another twenty-four hours.

She minimized the screen of her inbox and pulled up the file for the tree-lighting ceremony. She had so much to do today that, really, she should have enough to keep her mind occupied. But as she read the bids from the professional tree decorators, her mind invariably drifted to Nick.

How would he act once he had proof positive that he was the baby's father? Would he choose to be part of his child's life? Would he believe that despite their night together she didn't sleep around? Whatever he did, Becca fully intended to play the I-told-you-so card once she had the results in hand.

*Nice. That'll entice him to stay. It'll make you very pleasant to be around.*

She shook away the thought, clicked on her inbox and refreshed her browser again.

Still nothing.

So she picked up a red file folder that contained her notes for the ceremony.

"Good morning." Becca looked up to see Kate, dressed in a smart black pantsuit, holding a cup of coffee and standing in the doorway of her office.

"Hey," she said.

"Dare I ask?" Kate grimaced as if she were bracing for Becca to throw something at her. "Any news yet?"

Great. As if she needed any more nervous encouragement, but she knew Kate meant well. Becca didn't have the heart to sigh and tell her to go away. And to take her coffee with her.

Instead, she mustered her sweetest smile.

"Not yet."

Kate nodded, then took a sip from her mug. "Good coffee. You really are a saint for having it ready. Since you can't drink it, you really don't have to do that."

Becca closed the red folder. "I don't mind." She sipped her tea as if to prove she didn't need the high-octane fuel, and the fruity, spicy stuff served her much better.

"Come in for a minute." Becca pointed toward the chair. "Sit, please. Talk to me. Distract me. Stop me from checking my email at the top of every minute."

Becca happened to see the clock on the bottom right corner of her computer screen turn over to nine o'clock. So, she hit the refresh button once more.

"Okay, I did it again." Becca held up both hands, palms forward in surrender. "Stop me, please."

"Okay, Britney Spears. I wish there was some way I could rig your computer so that every time you check your email Britney would sing, 'Oops!… I Did It Again.' That would make you think twice, wouldn't it?"

"And how," Becca said.

"Of course, I could always come in here and sing to you every few minutes. A couple of rounds of Britney therapy will probably work like touching a hot stove. After you experience it, you just know better."

Becca laughed. "Darn, I wish I would've brought in the karaoke machine. I knew I was forgetting something."

"I'm happy to sing a cappella. That would probably have the biggest impact."

"Do you make house calls?" Becca asked. "I could've used you last night."

"Why? It was a little early to start the test result watch last night, wasn't it?"

"No, it wasn't that. I wasn't actually looking, but I was anxious about it. To take my mind off things, I let myself binge-watch classic movies. Turner Classics was having a James Dean film festival."

Kate narrowed her eyes and cocked her head to one side. "Sorry, hon, I'm not following you. Why is James Dean bad?"

*Why?* Becca shrugged.

"I know this sounds crazy, but there's something about Nick that reminded me of James Dean—with a modern spin and maybe with shades of Adam Levine and biceps and tattoos.

"But more rugged, though, less metrosexual," Becca added.

They paused for a moment of quiet appreciation, slow smiles spreading over their faces.

Actually, Becca had drawn the James Dean-Adam Levine parallel the first time she'd set eyes on Nick Ciotti. Well, actually, that's what she'd thought the second time she'd seen him. The first time, she hadn't really *seen* him. She'd been distraught over Victor's accident and the way Rosanna was trying to ice her out. She'd needed answers. But then when he'd walked into Bentleys, that's when she'd *seen* him.

After noting the James Dean comparison, her next thought had been that he had to be one of the best-looking human beings she'd ever laid eyes on. Bad-boy dangerous and take-your-breath-away gorgeous, with that shock of dark hair that was just a tad too long.

*Sigh.*

"I can totally see it," Kate said. "Did you sit and brood over James Dean last night?"

Becca tried to shrug it off. "I did and it's so stupid. I just need to get Nick out of my head. I keep going back and forth between being furious with him for pushing this paternity test issue and thinking that this guy and I are going to be irrevocably connected because of the baby. And despite it all, I want that. I really want it. But what he must think of me to insist on this test."

Kate looked at Becca for a long moment, and Becca could see the wheels turning in her friend's head.

*"What?"* Becca asked. "Just say what you're thinking. I've already admitted I'm a hot mess."

"I know it was hard for you to go get the test done. It probably felt as if he was questioning the very core of your character. I know that must've felt really crappy. But there are some women who—" Kate paused and winced. "How do I say this? Just don't hate me for it, okay?"

"Just say it."

"There are women out there who might try to trap a man like Nick."

"A man like Nick? What do you mean? I don't understand."

"He's a good-looking guy with a nice income and secure job. You know, a doctor."

"You sound like Jane Austen." In her best high-pitched British accent, Becca said, *"It is a truth universally acknowledged, that a single man in possession of a good fortune, must be in want of a wife."*

Kate laughed. "Well, not exactly. I was trying to say that there are certain women who think a man in possession of a good job, especially a doctor, would make a good husband. Okay, I guess that did sound a little Austen-ish. Remember Liam's neighbor Kimela Herring, and how she set her sights on him after his first wife passed away? That woman was shameless. She would've done anything—and I mean anything— to get her hooks in him. She's the reason I ended up bidding ten thousand dollars for him at that bachelor auction that funded the new pediatric wing at Celebration Memorial Hospital. Remember how she drove up the bid?"

Becca sat back in her chair and squinted at her friend while she tried to ignore the annoyance sparking in her solar plexus. "I remember, but I'm not quite sure where you're going with this trip down memory lane. Because surely you're not comparing me to Kimela Herring."

Kate looked genuinely surprised. Becca knew she sounded defensive, especially when Kate burst out laughing.

"Hardly," Kate said, a broad grin commandeering her face. "But what I am saying is, even though you are far from being a Kimela Herring and I know this is tremendously hard for you, you might want to cut Nick some slack. Women like Kimela throw themselves at men like Nick and Liam, and that might be one of the reasons Nick is so wary."

Becca wasn't quite sure what to say. She could always count on Kate to give it to her straight, but she was having a hard time swallowing what Kate was dishing up. Okay, so Nick was a doctor. That didn't make him better or worse than anyone. Even if certain women had a tendency to fling themselves at men like Nick. It certainly didn't absolve him of his responsibility.

Kate must've read that on her face, because she waved her hand as if she were erasing her words. "That didn't come out right. I feel like I just set back womankind two hundred years."

Becca cocked a brow. "Maybe three hundred years." But she smiled to let Kate know she wasn't taking it personally. She couldn't. Because even though Kate's words rankled her, Becca could step back and see that there was some truth to the matter. Gold diggers were real. They weren't the stuff of urban legends. She didn't like it, and she certainly didn't like the thought of Nick thinking of her that way.

"You're right," Becca said. "He doesn't know me."

"So please don't be too hard on him, or on yourself, for that matter, okay?" Kate said.

Becca offered a one-shoulder shrug but nodded. He'd see the truth soon enough. She wasn't trying to force his hand. Even if they were having a baby, she didn't want to marry a man she didn't love or a man who didn't love her.

For a moment her heart tried to eclipse logic with quiet protestations. How did she know she couldn't love Nick? She didn't even know him beyond that one earthmoving night, which proved that there had certainly been plenty of raw material to work with then.

*And, oh, how it had worked.*

As if the heavens were seconding that motion, a notice that she had a new email popped up on her computer screen.

She clicked over to her inbox.

The results were in.

After working the 7:00 p.m. to 7:00 a.m. shift the night before, which he would repeat tonight, Nick's days and nights were mixed up, but such was the life of someone employed in emergency medicine.

His schedule was as unpredictable as the cases that presented themselves each night in the ER. Some weeks he worked the graveyard shift, others he pulled the more civilized 8:00 a.m. to 8:00 p.m. one. Even though Celebration Memorial usually scheduled attendings four days on and three days off, sometimes the workweeks were longer, and he never knew what he'd be working one week to the next. That was fine because he was married to his job. Emergency medicine was a possessive spouse.

*But now he was going to be a father.*

He'd picked up Becca's text after he woke up around two o'clock. He hadn't even had a chance to grab a cup of coffee. So he was still a little groggy as he read the news. It was force of habit to check his phone the minute he rolled out of bed to make sure he was on top of things at the hospital, to make sure he hadn't missed an important call or text.

In this case, he had.

Becca had called. Then, when he'd slept right through that, she'd texted. Her message had said, The results are in. She'd included a link to a website and a password.

He'd known what the results would be before he'd typed in the first character. He'd known in his bones that Becca wasn't the kind of woman who would try to pawn off another guy's child on someone else. He supposed he'd known the truth since the moment he'd set eyes on her again in the emergency room, but he hadn't been able to wrap his mind around it.

A father. He was going to be a *father*. He couldn't imagine a worse person for such an important job. The kid deserved better than anything he could offer. Of course he would provide for the child, but love? How could he love someone else when he didn't even like himself sometimes?

The bald reality rolled around inside his gut, cold and heavy like a large ball bearing. To make it stop, he pushed up off the sofa bed and made short order of putting the couch back together, tossing the cushions into place. The chore had become a routine because if he didn't put away his bed, it dominated the living space in the tiny efficiency apartment that sat above George and Mary Jane Hewitt's garage. He'd rented the place on a month-to-month basis, figuring he'd find something more permanent once he got settled in his job and got to know the area. Since the place came fully furnished, he'd had the movers unload everything he owned, except his clothes, into a storage shed.

He didn't spend much time at home, and as the modest apartment came with everything he needed, he really hadn't missed the stuff that was stashed in those boxes. The Hewitts' granddaughter was coming to live with them in January. So they wouldn't offer more than a sixty-day lease. By that time, Nick figured he'd be settled in at the hospital and have a better read on the town. He'd even planned on looking up Becca.

It didn't make any sense to unpack only to pack it all up again when he moved again after the first of the year. It felt good and light and free to not be weighed down by worldly possessions, even if temporarily.

But he hadn't counted on the news that Becca was carrying his child.

*He was going to be a father.*

Maybe if he repeated the words to himself enough it would start to sink in. *Yeah.* No, that hadn't happened yet.

As Nick made his way into the tiny kitchenette, he uttered a silent oath that was utterly unfatherly. He braced his arms on the edge of the slip of kitchen counter, where the coffeemaker and toaster lived. He knocked his head against the cabinet in front of him for not being more careful.

But he had been careful. They'd used protection. Short of being celibate, how much more careful could he be?

The only thing that was crystal clear now was, with Nick as its father, this poor kid was screwed. Nick wasn't cut out to be a dad or a family man. The most devastating part of the equation was that this child hadn't asked for this, hadn't selected him. He or she—*God, this was a person, a living, breathing human being* whom he could screw up—deserved so much more than such a poor excuse for a father.

But like it or not, this child would arrive in about six months. There was no changing that. He squeezed his eyes together and raked both hands through his hair, which was still sleep mussed. Then he grabbed his phone and called Becca.

The phone rang three times, and he thought it might go to voice mail, but she answered.

"Hi, it's Nick."

There was a beat of silence, and for a moment he wondered if the call had dropped. He was just pulling the phone away from his ear to look at the screen when he heard her.

"Hi, Nick." Her voice sounded neutral, almost businesslike. Of course, she was probably at work. And nearly four hours had passed since she'd texted him this morning.

"I just picked up your text."

"Okay."

She wasn't going to make this easy on him, was she? Well, why should she?

Okay, so he had some smoothing over to do to convince her he wasn't a first-class creep. But he still felt justified asking for proof positive. He hoped Becca would understand that the test results were the first step in moving forward.

"We have a lot to talk about," he said.

"Do we, Nick?"

Her tone wasn't hostile, just calm, eerily calm, a matter-of-fact answer to his feeble attempts to meet her halfway.

"I would ask you to have dinner tonight, but I have to work at seven. Would you have time to meet for coffee after you get off work?"

"Meet me in Central Park in downtown Celebration at five o'clock."

He released a slow, controlled breath, both relieved and surprised that she'd agreed to see him. But she had, and that was the first step. They'd take it from there.

"I'll see you then."

"Nick," she said. "I don't expect you to marry me. So, don't worry."

What was he supposed to say to that? It was one of those damned if you do, damned if you don't situations, and he wasn't going there. This impassive front she was projecting was probably just a defense to gain control over a situation that felt way out of control. He felt out of control, too.

Becca had just told him he was off the hook. She'd just handed him a free pass. If he knew what was good for him, he'd take it and run. But he couldn't. And that made him feel so out of control it was as if his world was spinning, and all he could do was hang on or risk being flung off into parts unknown.

Actually, maybe that had already happened. Maybe this weird alternate universe was where he'd landed.

"I'll see you at five."

He arrived at the park a little early. He left his motorcycle in a parking space along the street and sat on a bench, looking at the fall decorations adorning the gazebo. Kids played in the park, running and laughing and chasing each other, as he sat there trying to gather his thoughts before Becca arrived.

Her words *I don't expect you to marry me* rattled in his brain. If Becca Flannigan was one thing, it was sincere. If she said it, she meant it. Nick knew he should've been relieved, but he wasn't. He wasn't sure what exactly he was feeling—

Until he saw her walking across the grass toward him in her red coat and boots. Something pinged in his gut. Awareness flooded his senses, and his body tightened in response.

An image of the night they were together played through his mind. A guy like him would be wise to ignore feelings like this. He shouldn't lead her on and make her think he was promising things he couldn't deliver. Becca and the baby deserved better than anything he had to offer. He had a history of tearing things apart, of ruining anything good that had ever come into his life.

She deserved to be married to the father of her child, if she wanted to be. Deserved to have a traditional family, a traditional life. The house with the white picket fence with dogs and cats in the yard, if that's what she wanted.

He didn't know for sure, because he didn't know her at all. Even if every cell in his body tried to convince him otherwise. As he stood to greet her, he shook off the unbidden memory of their night together—holding her, kissing her, making love to her. He had to man up and knock it off.

She offered a shy smile as she approached.

He had to fight the urge to hug her. He mentally scoffed. What the hell was wrong with him? He wasn't a hugger. He had to do something to lighten the mood and preempt the awkwardness.

"Go ahead and say it."

She squinted at him as she fidgeted with the scarf that hung around her neck. "Say what?"

"You can say *I told you so*. Twice if you want."

She nodded solemnly. "I thought about it, actually." She shrugged and looked away.

Maybe he shouldn't have tried to make a joke out of it. He was only trying to lighten the mood. A group of six preschool-aged kids ran ahead of their mothers, landing and tumbling in the grassy area directly in front of Nick and Becca.

Their mothers stopped at another bench about ten yards away and waved to Becca. She waved back. The three huddled for a moment, talking, then in unison they looked back at Nick and Becca. Then huddled up again.

"Friends of yours?" Nick asked.

"Acquaintances," she said. "I don't usually hang with the playgroup set. I guess that will change soon."

One of the kids, a little girl with white-blond curls,

let loose an earsplitting shriek, and two of her friends followed suit before they started chasing each other and shrieking even louder as they ran.

"Oh. Uh. Do you feel like walking?" he asked.

"Sure." Becca cast another glance at the three women and waved goodbye.

When they were safely out of earshot, Becca said, "This is so uncomfortable. So, I'm just going to say it and get it out into the open. I'm not going to force you to do anything you don't want to do, Nick. Neither of us planned this. And I know I've had more time than you to sit with this and come to terms with it, but I have to say, I'm happy now. I can't say I always was, but that night I was in the emergency room, I was so afraid I might lose the baby that it all suddenly became crystal clear. I want this child. I hope you'll be part of its life. I firmly believe a child, whether it's a boy or a girl, needs a father figure."

"Me? A father figure?" He shook his head. "Way out of my league. I would probably scar the poor kid for life. Maybe your dad or brother, if you have one, can be the father figure."

He meant it as a joke, something to lighten the mood. But she didn't laugh. She didn't even smile.

"Disregard that. It came out sounding wrong. I was trying to be funny, but I should know better."

"Just so you know, my parents don't know about the baby yet. Not many people do. Only you, Kate and maybe her husband, who also works at the hospital. But you don't have to worry about him saying anything to anyone."

"Who is he?" Nick asked.

"Liam Thayer. He's in charge of the hospital's pediatric unit."

"I haven't met him yet. But then again, I'm in my own little world in the ER unless a specialist consults. But Celebration isn't a very big town. Aren't you afraid, even if a couple of people know, word might get out before you tell your parents?"

"I trust Kate and Liam." She shrugged. "Telling my folks is easier said than done."

"You're a grown woman. What are you afraid of? It's your body and your life. Do you really care about what they think?"

"They're my parents, Nick. Of course I care."

"Sorry. That's a perfect example of just how bad I am at family relations."

"You're not close to your family?"

The question hit him like a punch to the gut. "No. I'm not."

"How come?"

He shook his head. "That doesn't really matter. Not right now, anyway. What is important is that you know that I will take responsibility for our child. I can't promise that I'll be a great father, but I will provide financially. I'm going to do what's right. You and the child will never want for a thing."

She stared at him with disappointed eyes.

"I don't understand why you're so sure you'd be a bad father."

"Once you get to know me, you'll understand."

She looked at him dubiously.

"For some reason I don't believe you. But you do bring up a good point. We need to get to know each other better."

One thing he was beginning to realize about Becca Flannigan was that she seemed to think the best of people. She saw the silver lining, when he tended to be too jaded to even see the clouds. He wasn't necessarily a pessimist. More of a realist.

But what could it hurt to get to know her better? After all, she was the mother of his child.

"That's a good idea. Since I'm just getting to know you and the town, maybe you can show me something that's typical of Celebration, Texas?"

He might've been imagining it, but he could've sworn he saw a half ton of tension lift from her shoulders. Those blue eyes of hers that could hypnotize him if he wasn't careful seemed to have regained some of their sparkle.

"I know you have to go to work. But I'll think of the most quintessential Celebration thing I can and let you know. But first, I have an appointment with my OB doctor tomorrow in Dallas. Will you go with me?"

His first thought was to say no, to back off—way off. But why should she have to go this alone? Especially after he'd just promised her that he would do what was right?

"Sure, let me know what time."

"Thank you. I'm so glad you're coming."

Before he knew what had hit him, she'd turned to him and hugged him. For a moment he didn't want to let her go.

## Chapter Four

The next day, Becca glanced around her obstetrician's office at all the happy pregnant couples who were in for appointments. There was a man and woman who were heartbreakingly tender toward each other. The husband—Becca guessed they were married because they wore matching wedding rings—sat with his arm protectively around his wife, gently stroking her shoulder.

If Becca had to wager, she'd bet that this was their first child, because they were young and seemed so much in love.

Another couple had brought their four kids with them. The little ones were playing in the children's area in the far corner of the office. Their father was sitting with them quietly keeping them in line.

As she glanced at Nick, who was sitting next to her reading a newspaper, she was torn. On one hand, she was happy he had agreed to come for the sonogram, but on the other, she felt like a fraud sitting there as if they were a couple who had conceived a baby as a by-product of their love. It shouldn't really matter. Nick was there, wasn't he?

He caught her staring, and he smiled at her, his eyes lingering on hers before they dropped down to her lips and then found their way back to his newspaper. She wasn't trying to fool anyone. They were here together because they were having a baby. Their relationship was nobody's business but their own.

Becca glanced around the waiting area at the posters adorning the walls—some featured tips on women's nutrition, there was a public service announcement that reminded women over thirty-five to get mammograms, and there was a watch-your-baby-grow poster addressing prenatal development and care.

Becca eyed the rendering of the three-month-old fetus. The poster said at this stage, her baby was about three inches long and had fingerprints.

Hmm. Only three inches? How could something so tiny make her feel so big already?

Becca's attention was momentarily shanghaied by a young woman who had just entered the office. She looked to be in her late teens or maybe early twenties, and she was very pregnant. She looked as if she might go into labor any moment. Becca noticed she wasn't wearing a ring on her left hand.

It shouldn't matter, but lately every time she saw a pregnant woman, she found herself looking at her left ring finger and sorting her into two categories: married and single.

She knew it was none of her business, and, yes, if she knew somebody was sorting her into categories, she probably wouldn't like it. But she wasn't judging. She just wanted proof that she wasn't the only one going this road alone.

Well, given the fact that Nick was here with her today, she wasn't exactly alone. But as much as the little voice inside of her wished it were different, they weren't a couple, either. They were certainly far from married.

After the young woman signed in, she turned and walked in Becca's direction. Her young face looked pale and drawn, as if she were exhausted down to her bones or maybe just plain weary. She was tall and waif thin, except for the basketball-sized baby bump protruding off her middle, which was visible only from the front and side. From the back, you couldn't even tell she was pregnant. She took a seat somewhere behind Becca, and if she wanted to continue watching her she'd have to turn around or relocate.

It was probably a good thing that she sat behind her, because Becca didn't want to stare. It was just that when she discovered a woman in the same situation she was, she felt an automatic need to bond with her—even if it was only with a smile of solidarity or an empathetic nod.

But this one had looked away as she had passed. Refusing to make eye contact. Probably because Becca had a man with her. As if on cue, Nick shifted his weight as he rested his elbow on the chair's armrest. His upper arm pressed against Becca's. The feel of his body pressed against hers caused heat to prickle a little on the back of her neck.

When he didn't immediately shift away, she gazed up at him, and he gave her a lopsided grin. The look in his eyes made her a little weak and melty on the inside, but she did her best to play it cool.

"Do you like football?" she asked.

He put down his newspaper and slanted her a glance, but his shoulder stayed right next to hers.

"I do."

She liked the warmth of his arm on hers. It made her think about how their bodies had felt skin to skin, and a little frisson shivered its way through her.

"I was thinking about how you wanted me to show you something typically Celebration. Maybe we could go to the football game Friday night. That is, if you're free. I know it's a weekend, and you might have to work or you might have plans."

She wondered if he was dating. Was there anyone else in his life?

Of course that's when the nurse chose to open the door and call them back into the exam room.

"Think about it," she said. "But no rush. You can let me know tomorrow."

Even though Nick was a doctor, he still felt a little out of place in the obstetrician's office. He wasn't sure what Becca had told them about him— the baby's father—the last time she'd been in for a checkup, but when she introduced him, the staff didn't seem to bat an eye.

Either it was commonplace for some fathers to not be involved, or the staff was very professional.

That helped him breathe easier. She shouldn't have to go this alone. Even if he wasn't much help. Maybe having someone there for support was something. Especially since she hadn't yet told her family. He, of all people, knew that sometimes family could be a bigger hindrance than help. Even though she hadn't said much, it sounded as if she and her folks had their challenges. That surprised him because Becca seemed warm and together, but maybe her family was as dysfunctional as his.

Nick's mind flashed back to his brother, Caiden, and that day when everything changed. The usual heavy feeling of guilt showed up and threatened to weigh him down, but he mentally shook away the thought. He wasn't going to bring his heavy baggage here. Today he was going to hear his child's heartbeat for the first time—maybe even see the sonogram picture.

With due respect to Caiden, he locked memories of his late brother in the recesses of his heart as he followed Becca through the maze of stations and stops, where they performed tests and took her vitals before finally showing them to an exam room.

"The doctor will be right in," said the nurse. "Make yourself comfortable."

Becca settled herself on the exam table. Nick didn't know how anyone could be comfortable sitting there.

"Are you sure you don't want the chair?" Nick asked, surprised by the protective feelings that had come to life inside him.

"Oh, no, thanks," she said. "I'm fine here. They'll do a sonogram. So I'll need to be on the table for that. I might as well stay here."

"How often do you have to come in for checkups?" he asked.

"Once a month right now, but the closer I get to my due date, the more often I'll have to come in. You're a doctor. You didn't know that?"

"In case I forgot to mention it, obstetrics isn't my specialty."

"Yeah, I think you mentioned it." She smiled at him. "Nick, I'm really glad you came with me today. I know this probably seems a little overwhelming, but having you here has made it so much easier for me."

"I haven't really done anything."

"Yes, you have. Just by being here."

She looked small and fragile sitting on that table. Nick had to fight the overwhelming urge to pull her into his arms and tell her he was willing to do anything he could to protect their child. But he didn't want to lead her on, and he didn't want to promise her anything he wasn't 100 percent certain he could deliver.

Memories of Caiden rattled that cage in the back of his mind, reminding him it probably wasn't in anyone's best interest—certainly not Becca's or the baby's—to promise more than financial support.

Becca had no idea how foreign the concept of family closeness was to him. Very few things scared him, but that was one of the things that did. Only because it was so big and so crucial—and in his experience, very unforgiving. One misstep and not only did you screw up your own life, but the person, the people who were counting on you, too...

*Stop. You're not doing this now.*

"By the way, I'm off Friday night," he said, taking his thoughts in a 180-degree turn.

Her face brightened. "Do you want to go to the football game?"

"That would be fun."

"It's a high school game. Is that okay? But the entire community turns out. I can't think of anything more typically Celebration than that."

"Sounds...fun."

"Did you play when you were in high school? Or even college?"

"Who, me?" He shook his head. "No. I didn't play sports."

"Too busy studying? When you were in high school, were you one of those übersmart guys who ruined the grade curve for everyone else?"

He'd ruined a lot of things for a lot of people when he was a teenager, but the bell curve wasn't one of them.

"No, I had to work much harder just to keep up. I had a part-time job that edged closer to full-time when I was in school, and then right after high school I joined the marines."

Her eyes widened, and her mouth formed an O. "Yet another thing I didn't know about you. You're a constant surprise, aren't you?"

He winked at her. "I try my best."

"Well, during football season the whole town shows up for Friday night football games. This year, Celebration High has a pretty good record. It's the first time since I can remember that they've been contenders for the district championship. It should be fun. I'm glad you want to go."

"What time does the game start?"

"Seven."

"Would you like to grab a bite to eat before the game?" he asked.

"That would be great. If you're up for the full experience, we could grab something there. The band boosters grill burgers and hot dogs and sell chips and sodas."

"Sounds like a meal fit for a king. How about I pick you up at six?"

Someone rapped on the door, and the doctor and his assistant entered the small room.

"Hello, Becca," he said. "How are we doing?"

He cast a curious glance at Nick, who was trying his best to disappear in the corner.

"Hi, Dr. Stevens. I'm feeling great, thank you. I'd like to introduce you to Dr. Nick Ciotti, the baby's father."

Nick recognized the practiced nonchalance with which Stevens greeted him. He was congenial, but there wasn't a trace of surprise that, at the three-month mark, Becca had finally produced the baby's phantom father.

After they shook hands and exchanged generic pleasantries, Becca told Stevens about the food poisoning and he got down to business asking her a series of questions.

"Have you felt the baby move yet?"

Becca shook her head. "No, not yet. Should I have already felt this?"

"No. Not necessarily. For a first pregnancy it could happen as early as fourteen weeks, but generally it happens between sixteen and twenty-five weeks."

"That's a wide range."

"Each pregnancy is as individual as the parents."

He asked her questions about morning sickness—she told him it had gone away; about fluid leakage and spotting—no to both; and whether she'd been taking her prenatal vitamins—religiously.

Then the doctor pulled over the fetal Doppler machine. Nick knew this machine because they had them in the emergency room. Dr. Stevens held a small probe against Becca's slightly rounded belly and moved it around until they could clearly hear the heartbeat.

The doctor listened for a moment and frowned.

"Is everything okay?" Nick asked.

The doctor moved the probe around more, seemingly lost in what he was doing.

"Dr. Stevens?" Becca said. "What's wrong?"

"Don't get your hopes up, because we need to do an ultrasound to confirm it, but I believe I hear two heartbeats. There's a chance that you might be pregnant with twins."

"Twins?" Her voice cracked. "I'd just gotten used to the idea of one child. And now Dr. Stevens confirms there are two babies. The rules keep changing on me here. Or should I say the reality keeps changing. And multiplying."

Nick smiled at her. The smile reached his eyes, making them crinkle at the edges. *Ooh*, those incredible hypnotizing brown eyes that looked darker and more soulful than ever right now.

"Obviously, I'm no expert, but I hear change is par for the course with children. Just when you think you have it all figured out, everything changes."

He shrugged.

"For someone who claims to know nothing about children, you sound pretty wise. Are you sure you're ready to do this?"

What a dumb question. They didn't really have any choice now. Or at least she didn't. She was still bracing herself, preparing for the moment that he changed his mind. And if learning that there was not one but two babies didn't send him running... She couldn't quite let down her guard and let herself go there yet.

"I don't see how either of us really has a choice," he said.

She couldn't read him. Or maybe she simply didn't want to because she couldn't handle any more changes until she digested the fact that they were having *twins*.

If it had thrown *her* for a loop, how in the world must he really be feeling?

An hour later, as they walked to the parking lot, the toe of Becca's boot caught an uneven edge of sidewalk and she did an awkward little stumble-dance to keep herself from falling.

An instant later, Nick's hand was around her waist steadying her. Her body was warm where he touched her. Or maybe it was just that the stumble had awakened the cymbal-banging monkey, and it was playing a wild staccato in her chest.

"I'm fine. Thanks." Her voice was a squeaky octave too high. She flashed him an awkward smile as heat crept up her cheeks, and she quickened her step away from him.

*Gaaa!* Leave it to her to be klutzy at the worst possible moment. She took a deep breath and blew it out as the burn of indignity taunted her.

"I guess I'd better get used to the uncertainty of parenthood," she said. "Just when I think I have it figured out, I realize I don't even know how I feel. I mean, I'm trying not to get too freaked out over his comment about twins making it necessary to classify the pregnancy *nearly normal*. Why? I should've asked questions, but I was too stunned. Now that everything is sinking in, I have a million questions. I'm going to stew about them until my next appointment. Do you know what he meant by *nearly normal*?"

"Do you want to go back in and ask him?"

"I hate barging back in. It would throw off their schedule. I'll call them tomorrow."

"He mentioned that Southwestern Medical Center specializes in high-risk deliveries. I can check into it for you—for us."

Nearly normal pregnancy. High-risk delivery. Just hearing the words made her head swim.

She was so glad Nick had come to the appointment with her, and good grief, how would she be feeling right now if he'd left her to go this alone?

She needed to at least pretend as if she was in control of her emotions. But her body still tingled where he'd touched her, and a tear had leaked out of the corner of one eye and was meandering down her cheek, and then another one followed. She tried to take a deep breath, but it sounded so shuddering and pathetic.

She attempted to turn away before Nick could see how ridiculous she was being, but before she could, he'd caught her and had drawn her back into his arms.

"It's going to be okay," he said. "Let's just take this one step at a time. I promise I will do everything in my power to make sure you don't have to worry about anything."

His words were soothing, and she stayed in his

arms until she had regained her composure. She pulled back a little to wipe her eyes, but first she looked up at him. His gaze snared hers, and then he was looking at her mouth, and she was leaning into him.

When he took her chin in his hand and drew her closer, she felt his warm, mint-scented breath so near that every feeling—every dream and desire she'd had since the first moment she'd set eyes on him that night at the hospital—played out before her eyes. Since then, since learning she was pregnant, since finding him again, one of the things she tried not to think about was the way his arms would feel around her, protective and strong. The way his lips would taste… That taste that was so uniquely Nick.

Then he kissed her. Despite everything, the kiss surprised her. The tentative touch and softness of his lips were a sexy contrast to his masculinity—even better than she remembered from that night at Bentleys. The warmth lingered, melting the chill in the air. His mouth was so inviting, and even though a voice of reason sounded in a distant fog in the back of her mind, saying she really shouldn't be doing this, she couldn't quite make herself stop.

He pulled her closer, enveloping her in his arms.

Again, he dusted her lips with a featherlight kiss, as if he were trying to kiss away all of her doubt and insecurity. When his mouth finally covered hers, he kissed her with such an astonishing passion, she was sure it had to have come from his soul.

It was a deep, demanding kiss, and it sent all of her senses reeling and let loose a yearning that consumed her entire body. The way he touched her—one hand in her hair, holding her protectively in place, while the other slid down, caressing her back, edging its way underneath the hem of her blouse until the skin-on-skin contact made it too hard for her to catch her breath.

A low groan of desire broke through the sounds of the cars whooshing by on the highway and a horn honking in the distance. She realized the moan had come from her. If she knew what was good for her, she'd stop now before she got too attached to this man who might or might not choose to be in her life—and even if he did stick around, he might want things to be strictly platonic. Unlike this very *not* platonic kiss.

She pulled back, muttering something about it being late and needing to go and not wanting to keep him from the hospital.

She knew the contrast was jarring, and she saw the confusion on Nick's face as she drove away. When she looked in her rearview mirror, he was still standing there watching her.

## Chapter Five

Nick paid for their football tickets, and they entered the gates at Denison Field. She hadn't been to many football games lately, but the field looked exactly the same as when Becca had gone to Celebration High School.

It was hard to believe it had been seven years since she'd graduated. Yet stepping through those gates it felt as if she were transported back in time. She had gone away to college at the University of Florida, and yet she'd chosen to return to her hometown.

Celebration was a place like no other. Even though everybody knew everything about everyone in town— for the most part, though she'd managed to keep her pregnancy a secret, for now, anyway—it was nice to be part of something bigger than she was, something exactly like this town.

"Welcome to Denison Field," she said to Nick. They had arrived a half hour before the game was supposed to start, and the place was already filling up. "I spent a lot of time here as a teenager. As you can see, the whole town turns out for the games. Especially when the team is doing well."

She laughed.

"Everybody loves a winner," Nick said.

"Don't they, though?"

Becca inhaled the scent of flame-grilled burger. "*Mmm*, smell that? It's the best burger in town."

The left side of Nick's mouth turned up in a sardonic grin. "If the best burger in town is cooked by a bunch of band parents, should I be worried about my new hometown?"

"Absolutely not. The dads have gotten together and they run a food truck on weekends to raise money for the band. They've managed to buy a fleet of new tubas and outfit seventy-five kids with brand-new marching uniforms."

"That's enterprising. I hope they can cook as well as they can fund-raise."

"Are you kidding? Apparently, the burger recipe is one that Stubby Blanchard's great-grandmother came up with decades ago. Rumor has it that Ray Isaac, the chef at Bistro St. Germaine, offered to buy the recipe and exclusive rights from Stubby, but Stubby wouldn't sell. Now Ray has made it his mission to figure out the recipe on his own. The town has been calling it burger wars. The funny thing is, even though Ray graduated from Le Cordon Bleu in Paris, he can't seem to figure it out."

"It's probably some strange ingredient we'd never think of, like peanut butter or baking soda," said Nick.

"Baking soda? Don't say that out loud around Stubby. Because he gets uneasy about people trying to deconstruct his burger—and baking soda?"

First, Becca made a face, and then she shrugged. "Watch the secret ingredient turn out to be just that!"

"Becca Flannigan? Is that you?"

Becca turned to see Lucy Campbell, an old high school friend she hadn't seen since graduation.

"Lucy! How are you? When did you get back into town?"

"Just last week. I moved back from California. I went out there to try my hand at starting my own fabric line."

"You always were so artistic," Becca said. "How did it go?"

"Well, the cost of living is so high, I had to take another job to support myself, and it was difficult enough to find time to devote to my designs, much less take time off work to meet with potential investors. So I decided to move back and concentrate on my art. And who's this?"

Lucy all but batted her lashes at Nick. He seemed to have that effect on women.

"Lucy Campbell, this is Nick Ciotti. Lucy and I were good friends in high school. I can't believe we lost touch over the years."

Lucy offered Nick her hand; Nick shook it.

"Nice to meet you," he said.

"Nice to meet you, too, Nick. *Sooo*—" Lucy looked back and forth between Becca and Nick. "Are you two dating?"

The subtext to Lucy's question was *is Nick taken or is he fair game?* Even though Becca knew that Lucy was a harmless flirt, she couldn't help but feel a tad territorial. Because the truth was she didn't know what to say.

*Actually, Lucy, tonight is our first date. Unless you count going to the obstetrician together and the night we slept together three months ago when I didn't even know his last name. Oh, did I mention that we're having a baby? Actually, we're having two babies. Twins!*

Good Lord.

Not unless she wanted the news broadcast all over town. Sure, Lucy was harmless, but it was the rare soul in this town who could keep a juicy secret like good-girl Becca Flannigan getting knocked up. Especially if they were the one who got to break the news.

Becca figured the best way to head off the question was simply not to answer it.

"Lucy, it was great to see you. We need to run, but let's get together sometime soon and catch up. Okay?"

Maybe by then she would know what to say. Because right now she hadn't given up hope that maybe she and Nick might figure it out and make it work. The thought cued the cymbal monkey in her chest, and it began banging away again.

Becca gauged right. Lucy had enough class to know better than to push the question.

"Absolutely," she said. "I can't wait to catch up. I'm staying with my sister until I get settled. You remember Hannah, don't you?"

Becca nodded.

"Let me give you my cell number." As Lucy rattled off the number, Becca added it to the contacts in her cell. "Please, give me a call, and we can set up something."

Becca was never so glad to get away from anyone. As she and Nick walked away, the sinking feeling hit her that bringing him here had probably been a bad idea. A very bad idea. How the heck had she figured she and Nick would get lost in the crowd when every night at a Celebration High School football game was like homecoming? Especially when most of the people in town had never met Nick and probably thought she didn't even date.

She wondered for a moment if it was too late to suggest that they do something else. In fact, she glanced up at him ready to ask him if they could leave, but his eyes met hers, and in that split second she didn't care if the two of them stayed or went. She didn't care if people asked questions or wanted to meet the new guy.

Things would work themselves out the way they were meant to.

But tonight, he was there with her.

That was all that mattered.

"I noticed how you evaded her question," Nick said. He looked as if he was trying not to laugh.

"You think it's funny, huh? What was I supposed to say?"

Her heart dared her to tack on the words *boyfriend*, *fiancé*, *baby daddy*, but her mouth chickened out.

"Actually, I thought it was pretty skillful."

"And I noticed that you just skillfully evaded my question," she said.

He smiled at her again. "Did I? I guess I didn't understand the question."

"I'll give you that. It's sort of a hard one to understand, isn't it?"

Thank God the color announcers chose that moment to inform the crowd that tonight was senior night and that the football players, cheerleaders and band members would have their photos taken on the field with family members during the halftime break.

"Oh, shoot," Becca said. "I completely forgot it was senior night."

"Did you forget you were supposed to have your picture taken at halftime?" Nick teased. "After we get our food, I'll hold your cheeseburger for you if you need to go freshen up. Although if it's as good as you say it is, I can't guarantee it'll still be here when you get back."

"Very funny. My nephew Kevin is on the football team, and he's a senior."

"You have two nephews? Victor, the one who was in the emergency room that night, and Kevin?"

"Three, actually, and a niece. Victor belongs to my sister. Kevin and Marshall, who is a junior, are my brother Mark's sons. They're all on the football team. My niece, Nora, who is Mark's daughter, is a cheerleader." She waved it away. "I have a big, complicated family. If my sister realizes I'm here and I avoided the photo, it could cause a pretty bad scene. But the funny thing is, if I wanted to be in the photo, she would probably find a reason that I shouldn't. You remember my sister? She's the one who threw me out of the emergency room the night we met."

"Oh, right. I do remember her. She was kind of scary. Although, I have thought about thanking her for throwing you out, because if she hadn't…"

Oh. *Oh!*

Becca could read a whole lot into that. Again, her brain wanted her to ask him if he realized that if Rosanna hadn't been in such a rage that night, they probably wouldn't be expecting twins next May. But her mouth couldn't ask the question. And if she couldn't ask the question, he couldn't refute or clarify exactly what he meant, and she could go on believing that he was happy they *met*.

Thank goodness her parents wouldn't be there tonight. She wouldn't have suggested going to the game if she thought they'd be here.

They never went to the games when the temperature dipped below sixty degrees, which it was tonight and most Friday nights in November. Her mother had suffered a case of pleurisy ten or fifteen years ago. The cold aggravated the condition—even after all this time. Becca suspected Isabel used it as an excuse to avoid certain functions—such as football games, which were at the bottom of her mother's list of fun things to do, along with root canals and gynecologist appointments.

Of course, Rosanna would be there because Victor was second-string varsity. He didn't play much, if at all, but it was rare for a freshman to make the varsity team. Even if he rode the bench, he did it proudly. Rosanna would be holding court in the bleachers with the other football moms.

Since it would be shoulder-to-shoulder crowded, Becca didn't worry about running into Mark and Rosanna. And, honestly, it wouldn't be the end of the world if she did. She'd simply introduce Nick and tell them—tell them what?

* * *

As they made their way toward the concession area, Becca saw Kate and Liam heading toward them. Kate's eyes flashed, and a broad smile overtook her face when she caught sight of them.

"You're here," she said, greeting Becca with a warm hug.

"We are," said Becca. "Nick asked me to show him something quintessentially Celebration. Since the entire population of the town will be here tonight, I thought I would give him Celebration in one fell swoop."

"You're a brave man, Dr. Ciotti," said Liam. "I didn't attend my first game until my daughters made the cheerleading squad."

They all looked down at the track.

"Amanda and Calee are so excited to be cheering with Nora this year," Kate said. "Nora is Becca's niece. Did she tell you? And her nephews are on the team."

"She did," Nick said.

"Ooh, I can't watch." Kate gestured toward the cheerleaders. They were organizing to do one of their stunts. Nora and one of Kate and Liam's girls were at the base of the pyramid holding the leg of Liam and Kate's other daughter, who was teetering high on top.

Becca winced right along with her. "They're adorable and so athletic, but I can't watch them do those stunts. I'm always so afraid they will fall and get hurt."

Kate sighed. "But their coach is all about safety. So we've all agreed that as long as they're vigilant and they play by the rules, we won't embarrass them by hiding our eyes when they perform stunts and acrobatics."

"We'd rather them be here than out who knows where." Liam slid his arm around Kate's shoulders. "Not that we would let them go to *who knows where*, but it is good that they are involved in something that takes up so much of their time."

Kate had married into her ready-made family and adopted Amanda and Calee when she and Liam wed. Liam had lost his wife in a tragic accident, and both he and the girls had benefited from Kate's nurturing touch.

"Are you two coming over on Sunday night?" Kate asked, directing her question mostly toward Nick.

"What's going on Sunday night?" Nick said.

"You are new to the area, aren't you?" Liam teased.

"Every Sunday night we get together to watch the Dallas Cowboys play football. Well, the guys watch the game, and the ladies usually gather in the dining room. This week, we're making wedding favors for Anna Adams and Jake Lennox's wedding. You might know them from the hospital. Anna is a nurse, and Jake is an attending."

"Right. I met them on my first day at the hospital, actually," said Nick.

"Well, then, in addition to football on Sunday night, you might want to mark the Sunday of Thanksgiving weekend on your calendar."

"Is the whole town invited?"

"Pretty much," said Kate. "A lot of people from the hospital are on the guest list. I hope you have a nice suit. You can be Becca's date."

Becca felt her face heating up. She wished she

could grab one—or maybe she'd need two—of her niece's pom-poms so she could stuff them in Kate's mouth to shut her up.

"Since I'm the new guy, I'll probably get the honor of working that night. Someone will have to hold down the fort."

"We will have to see about that," said Kate. She flashed a smile that Becca knew meant *you can thank me later.* "They've made arrangements for the shifts to be covered."

"We'd better find a seat before kickoff," said Liam. "If we stay here much longer, this one will be planning your wedding."

"Okay, let's hear it for my friends Mr. and Mrs. Awkward, guaranteed to make everyone feel uncomfortable. We're going now. Bye-bye."

"You're welcome to sit with us," Liam called after them.

"Thank you, but if we wanted to be tortured all night, my sister is right over there." Becca gestured with her head toward the crowd in the center of the bleachers, the area that was reserved for the Celebration Quarterback Club. Then she hooked her arm through Nick's and steered him away.

"See you Sunday," Kate called.

Becca waved goodbye without looking back at her friends. She knew Kate and Liam meant well, and she wasn't mad at them for being so forward. In fact, Becca hoped Kate hadn't scared off Nick and that he wanted to come to the football gathering Sunday night. The five couples who got together every Sunday night in the fall were some of her best friends.

Over the years she'd watched them meet and marry their sweethearts. She was the last single in the bunch.

Now that she thought about it, if Nick didn't want to come, she wasn't going to push him. The two of them would be the lone singles swimming in the sea of married couples. That would levy an altogether different kind of pressure than what Kate and Liam had joked about tonight.

Once they were a good distance away, Becca withdrew her arm from Nick's.

"I'm sorry about that," she said.

"About what?" he asked.

His question threw her for a moment, but she recovered.

"They love to joke around. The football parties are fun. It's a great excuse for everyone to get together. I don't want you to get the wrong idea and think that it would be a night full of pressure, of them pushing us together. It's mostly guys in one room and women in another—especially this week, since we'll be busy with the wedding favors. With as many people as Jake and Anna are inviting, it's going to take a village to get them done on time."

Before he could answer, they walked into the midst of a rush of latecomers who had just purchased tickets and were streaming into Denison Field, obviously intent on getting to the bleachers to find seats before kickoff. Becca and Nick were momentarily separated. But once Becca found her way through the crowd, Nick was waiting on the other side for her. Her stomach did a little stutter-step—as it did every time she saw him. There was this momentary rush of disorientation over the fact that this gorgeous man—this man who looked dark and a little bit dangerous—was actually very kind and caring, even if he was still a bit of a mystery.

Nick knew Kate and Liam's good-natured banter was just that—good-natured banter. He also knew they wouldn't say things like that if they didn't welcome him into their inner circle. Sure, there was a grain of seriousness to it, and if he let it, it might bother him—only because he wasn't used to other people being so into his business. But as he looked around at all of the people who'd turned out tonight for the football game, he realized living in a small town like Celebration meant people would be in your business. It was a given. Celebration wasn't like San Antonio, where it was easy to be a face in the crowd. Here, new faces stood out in the crowd, and the community made it their business to find out about their new neighbor.

His gaze snared Becca's as she walked toward him. Someone stopped her and greeted her with a hug. It gave Nick a chance to watch her without her realizing he was staring. She looked gorgeous in her tight jeans and blue-and-white Celebration High School Wildcats spirit shirt. Her navy blue peacoat hung open so that the T-shirt underneath was visible. He couldn't help but notice how the V-neck emphasized her breasts, which had been sexy as hell before the pregnancy, and appeared to be even fuller now.

A man would have to be dead not to notice how good she looked. And damned if that same aching need that had drawn him to her that first night didn't threaten to consume him again.

When she reached his side, he took her hand. "We wouldn't want to get separated again. I might not be able to find you amid the throng of sports fans here tonight."

She smiled at him, and they found their way to the small outbuilding to the right of the bleachers where the band boosters were selling food.

The smell of grilled burgers and hot dogs filled the air, and Nick's stomach rumbled. He wasn't sure the concessions would feed what he was hungry for, but for now it would have to do. They got in line just in time for the marching band to begin playing "The Star-Spangled Banner." All of the cooks put down their spatulas and removed their hats; the money takers stood and put their hands over their hearts. Everything stopped until the piccolos trilled the last trill and the cymbals put the final exclamation point on the national anthem.

When it was all over and the announcer started speaking, Becca asked, "What are you going to have?"

He smiled at her, tempted to say, *The same thing I had that night at Bentleys.* But she had acted so jumpy over Liam and Kate's teasing that he didn't want to push it.

Right now, he was content to be out with her on this beautiful, cool fall evening, holding her hand and enjoying her company.

"I think I'll have a cheeseburger and fries. They must be serious if they're operating their own Fry-Daddy."

"Best fries in town. I highly recommend them."

The crowd went wild as the team ran out onto the field. The announcer informed everyone that if the

Wildcats won the game tonight they would advance to the semifinals for the district championship. The crowd cheered again, and several people leaned on air horns. The band broke into a rousing round of what must've been the school's fight song. After another exuberant cheer, the crowd settled down until the Wildcats won the coin toss and elected to kick the ball to the visiting team.

"It's nice that the town supports the team so well," Nick said. "I guess in its own way Celebration isn't really the sleepy little town that I thought it would be."

"No, the people around here tend to make their own fun. It may not be a wild party—unless you come over to Kate and Liam's for football Sunday—but it's nice."

It was nice. It was everything he imagined being part of a small community would be. He wasn't exactly sure how he felt about that. If truth be told, the small-town closeness was one of the reasons he had turned down the job in the first place. But when they came back with an offer he couldn't refuse, well, he simply couldn't refuse.

They ordered their food—two cheeseburgers, two orders of fries, a bottle of water for Becca and a can of cola for himself—and made their way over to a group of high-top patio tables that were off to the side but still allowed them a partial view of the field.

Since most of the people in attendance had crowded into the bleachers, the area where they enjoyed their meal was mostly empty except for a small knot of teenagers who obviously had no interest in watching the game.

"Does Kate know about the latest development in our little adventure?"

"No, we were busy today, and… I don't know. I guess I'm still getting my head wrapped around our growing family."

"Rebecca?"

The voice came from behind him, so he couldn't see who it was, but good grief this woman was popular. Granted, Celebration was a small town; Becca Flannigan obviously knew everyone who had ever lived here.

But he only had to take one look at her face to realize she wasn't thrilled to see this person.

Nick turned around and saw an impeccably dressed woman with the same basic bone structure and clear blue eyes as Becca. At that moment he caught a glimpse of what Becca might look like in twenty-five or thirty years. This had to be Becca's mother. The distinguished man with silver hair at her side had to be Becca's father.

"Rebecca, you're here. Good. I meant to call you today to remind you that tonight is senior night, and Kevin is getting a family portrait made on the field, and we all need to be in the picture. Make sure you meet us at the half."

The woman stopped abruptly and trained those piercing blue eyes on Nick. The way she tilted back her head gave her the appearance of looking down her aquiline nose.

"Rebecca, who is this? Please, introduce your friend to us."

Even though it was more of a command than a request, Nick stood. "Hello, Mr. and Mrs. Flannigan, I'm Nick Ciotti. Very nice to meet you."

As he greeted Becca's mother and shook her father's hand, some of the missing pieces to the puzzle fell into place.

While the Flannigans were cordial, they were also a bit cold and aloof. The way they carried themselves and the way they dressed suggested affluence. Nick could see through the stuffy, polite veneer to the judgmental subtext lurking below.

Later at halftime, as he stood at the chain-link fence that separated the track and football field from the bleachers, he watched the dynamics among the Flannigan family. As Becca joined her nephew's senior night photograph, he realized that he and perfect, beautiful Becca Flannigan were more alike than he'd realized. Even though she was part of a big, wealthy family—the opposite of his working-class parents— he sensed that Becca felt just as alone in the world as he did.

## Chapter Six

Two nights later Becca sat at Kate's dining room table sipping caffeine-free pumpkin spice chai tea and chatting with five of her best girlfriends as they filled mini mason jars with monogrammed candy.

Anna and Jake had gotten engaged over the summer and had planned on getting married the following spring, but Regency Cypress Plantation and Botanical Gardens, which was booked out for nearly two and a half years, had an unexpected cancellation, and Anna and Jake had been able to grab it.

The only problem was now all plans were on the fast track, and it really was taking all hands to pull off the wedding of Anna's dreams.

Two weeks ago, the six of them had sat at this very dining room table stuffing, addressing, sealing and stamping invitations to three hundred of the couple's close friends. The available date, November 29, was one week from today—the Sunday of Thanksgiving weekend. It wasn't ideal, since so many people went away for the holiday and traveled on that Sunday.

Because of the time crunch, the girls were under strict instructions that they could not leave Kate's house tonight until they'd each filled fifty jars.

As an incentive, Anna had offered to buy dinner for the person who finished first and helped the slow-poke of the group get up to speed.

Becca knew she might very well end up being the slowpoke tonight because her mind was elsewhere. She loved her friends, but tonight, she wanted to be a fly on the wall in the living room, where Nick was bonding with the guys.

He'd surprised her and agreed to come with her to Kate and Liam's tonight. After the arm twisting the night before last, Becca made up her mind not to push him. She couldn't think of a faster way to scare off a man than to guilt him into spending a Sunday evening with her friends.

But if the sounds coming from the living room were any indication, her friends were becoming his friends. That made her happy beyond words. Still, a fly on the wall had no use for words. So she kept her head down and her ear tuned in, trying to pick out Nick's voice among the mix of hooting, hollering and the occasional bit of hospital talk, since four of the six men were doctors.

"Who needs more wine?" Pepper hopped up and started going around the table refilling goblets with the bottle of Chianti she'd brought back from Italy.

"Becca, honey, why are you drinking that god-awful caffeine-free tea when you could be enjoying a little piece of Italian heaven. Here, let me get you a glass."

"No, thanks, Pepper. I'm good."

Pepper laughed. "How could anybody be good drinking that liquid spice ball?"

When Pepper headed off into the kitchen, Becca and Kate exchanged a look. Pepper was a sweetheart, but sometimes she could be too damn bossy for her own good. Or in tonight's circumstances, for Becca's good.

The woman was like a bloodhound—she could smell a secret two counties over. And Pepper's antennae had been up since Becca's trip to the emergency room after her bout of food poisoning. Pepper hated feeling left out. However, she was a Southern belle, and rather than ferreting out the answer she was looking for, she used techniques that involved endearment, helpfulness and graciousness—key tools of the Southern belles trade.

Tonight she would obviously not rest until Becca either drank the Chianti or served up a Pepper-approved explanation as to why she was passing on such a treat.

When she came back into the dining room, she set the glass in front of Becca and drained the rest of the bottle into it. As soon as Pepper had finished, Kate waltzed right over and swooped up the wine.

There was hierarchy at work here. Pepper was married to Kate's brother, Rob, and as the sister-in-law, Kate could get away with certain transgressions that mere mortals would never in their right minds dream of committing.

"Kate, darling, if you would like some more wine, I brought another bottle. We can open it. Granted, it's not from Italy, but I do so want Becca to try the Chianti. I don't want her to miss out."

Kate had done her part. Becca had to think fast.

"It's very sweet of you, Pepper, but I haven't felt like myself all day long. I'm afraid if I have even a taste of wine it might not settle with me. It doesn't even sound good right now. So I'd hate for you to waste it on me."

There. That was good. Only a social moron would keep pushing wine on a person who wasn't feeling well. Becca was glad to get Pepper off of her back, because she certainly couldn't tell anyone else about the babies until she told her parents.

Kate was a rare, reliable jewel, and Becca knew her secret was safe with her. Kate was more reliable than a Fort Knox vault.

"You're not pregnant, are you?" A.J. laughed at her own joke. Their friends Lily and Anna joined in the merriment because on a normal day Becca would've been voted the least likely of all the women at the table to announce she was carrying twins.

"Good one, A.J.," Becca said. "How many glasses of wine has she had tonight? I hope Shane is driving."

Then the doorbell rang.

"I'll get it." Becca stood to answer it. Kate seemed to instinctively understand that answering the door was Becca's chance to escape the inquisition. On her way, as she passed by the living room, she would also be able to glance in and see how Nick was getting along.

Nick caught her looking. She was glad, too, because even though there was a football game on the television and an abundance of testosterone in the room, he'd been in tune enough to her presence that he'd sensed her coming. Or more likely she just got lucky and happened by when he happened to be looking up.

She relished the breathless excitement, the way the mere sight of him made her stomach flip. She shot him a flirty little smile that was as much eyes as it was lips and kept right on walking to the front door.

She'd been so wrapped up in flirting with Nick, and since the usual gang was present and accounted for, she hadn't given much thought to who might be at the door.

Before Becca could actually open the door, the person on the other side let himself in. Becca found herself face-to-face with Zane Phillips, a friend of Rob's and whose own horse-breeding ranch was located about ten miles outside of Celebration. The guy was tall and rich and all kinds of gorgeous.

"Zane, hello. What a surprise. I didn't realize you were coming over."

Zane flashed her his trademark rugged, sexy smile. "Hello, Becca. I certainly am glad to see you. I had no idea that you were part of this football party or I would have joined in a lot sooner."

Last year, Zane had hosted a fund-raiser for the foundation on his ranch. At one time, Becca would have given her eyeteeth for him to ask her out. Today, as she stood there in the foyer with him acting all attentive and flirty, all she could think about was Nick.

"Come in. The guys are in the living room."

Zane lingered in the foyer. He didn't seem very worried that he was missing the game.

"How have you been?" he asked. "And why did we never go out after the fund-raiser?"

Wow. Her timing really did stink. Actually, Zane was the one with bad timing.

"If I remember correctly, it's because you had a girlfriend."

He held his index finger in the air. "You have a very good memory."

"It comes in handy sometimes."

"And, apparently, a good sense of humor, too. I don't have a girlfriend anymore. Apparently, she didn't have a very good sense of humor."

Was he about to ask her out? Right here? In the middle of Kate and Liam's foyer? Six months ago this would been something from a dream. But now Becca found herself inwardly squirming and backpedaling faster than a unicyclist poised to ride over a cliff.

"Can I get you a beer, Zane?"

Maybe she could buy herself a little time by offering him some liquid refreshment. Then Nick stepped from the living room into the foyer.

"I was just going to get myself one, Becca," Nick said. "Would you help me find the kitchen?"

Could the man—Zane someone or the other—not take a hint?

Nick knew he had no right or claim on Becca, even though she was pregnant with his babies.

Still, in his book, when a guy was late to the party and it was clear that a certain woman was there with another guy, the latecomer needed to back the hell up and stop flirting.

Was he jealous?

Was that what this foreign feeling was? Jealousy? He'd never experienced it before—or at least not like this.

Nick tried his best not to let it show as he followed Becca into the kitchen, even though Zane hadn't seemed to pick up on the subtle hint and trailed along behind them.

"How is the favor making going?"

Becca ducked her head and lowered her voice. "It would be fine if Pepper would stop pushing wine on me."

"Seriously?" he asked.

She grimaced. "Yes. I can't tell if she's just in a generous mood, wanting me to share in the wine she brought back from Italy, or if she's onto something and trying to force my hand. Know what I mean?"

Nick blew out an audible breath. "Sorry about that."

"Thanks, but it's not your fault. She can be a little bulldog when there's something she wants to know and feels like it's being kept from her."

"We can leave anytime you want," Nick said as they stepped into the kitchen.

Just like the rest of Liam and Kate's home, the kitchen was traditional and expensive-looking with its marble countertops and stainless-steel appliances. Yet, with pictures and progress reports and notes tacked to the refrigerator and silly messages and re-minders scrawled on the chalkboard that hung by the door, it still had a lived-in look that suggested this room was the heart of the Thayer family.

Liam and Kate's two girls, who had been cheering at the game Friday night, were hanging out with Lily and Cullen's brood of children, whom the couple had adopted shortly before they got married, Nick had heard. Cullen, who was chief of staff at Celebration Memorial, had been the kids' godparent before their natural parents had died in a car accident. The older kids were watching A.J. and Shane's toddler.

Everything about this group seemed to be centered around family. That concept was so foreign to Nick, but in a strange way it almost felt as if he could trust them to be a built-in support system for him and Becca—once they broke the news.

Still, the jaded, scarred part of him that had always relied on himself warned him not to be so trusting so fast. Periods of flux sometimes had people swimming for what they thought was the surface, but when it was too late they realized they were actually heading in the wrong direction.

"Aren't you having a good time?" Becca asked.

"I'm having a great time. But I don't want you to be uncomfortable."

"That's very sweet," Becca said. She touched his hand, and the urge to kiss her again had him lacing his fingers in hers.

The way she looked into his eyes made him believe that she wanted that, too. And for a moment he'd almost forgotten about Zane, who'd made a detour through the dining room to flirt with the other women, no doubt. They were married women, but the guy didn't seem to care.

For a moment Nick gave the guy the benefit of the doubt. Maybe he was just one of those men who loved women. Couldn't fault him for that. Especially since the detour seemed to indicate that he must have gotten the hint that Becca wasn't available—at least not tonight.

And then the guy made his presence known.

"Hey, what are you two conspiring about? The way you have your heads together makes me wonder if there's something I need to know."

*You need to know what we're talking about is none of your business. You need to know that you should back off. You need to know that Becca obviously isn't into you—*

"How about those beers, guys?" Becca said, her voice a lot perkier than it had been just moments before.

Nick held up a hand. "Thanks, but I'm good. I don't need to drink any more tonight, since I'm driving you home."

He wished he could take back that last part, but he couldn't help saying it. When would Zane finally get the hint? The guy had asked her out, and she hadn't answered; he'd noticed that the two of them had had their heads together in private conversation; and now Nick had made it very clear that he was the one taking her home.

Anyone with half a brain would catch the hint.

"I didn't even introduce you two," Becca said, suddenly all good manners and charm. "Nick, Zane is a good friend of Pepper's husband, Rob. He has been a big supporter of the Macintyre Family Foundation. He has sponsored a couple of fund-raisers for us. Zane, Nick is new in town. He's a doctor in the emergency room at Celebration Memorial. He's been here less than a month. I know I can count on you to make him feel welcome."

After a long pause, Zane extended his hand. "Welcome to Celebration, Nick. It's a great place."

As Becca got a beer out of the refrigerator, Liam entered the kitchen, carrying four empty beer bottles.

"There you are, Nick. It's halftime. Tell me more about your thoughts on the Hastings kid."

Nick watched Becca hand the bottle to Zane.

"Austin Roberts told me the boy has been in twice for chest pains over the past ten days," Nick said. "In between ER visits, he was treated by his family doctor, who diagnosed an upper respiratory infection. I heard that he was back in the ER last night. Was he tested for aortic dissection?"

Liam placed the bottles on the counter near the sink and turned back to Nick, a solemn expression on his face.

"I don't know. He's only sixteen years old. That disorder is not very common in people so young."

"Any family history of aortic dissection?"

"I couldn't tell you without his chart here in front of me, but I'll contact his pediatrician and see if he thinks tests are warranted."

"I suppose that's all we can do right now, since he has a pediatrician."

It went against protocol to question another doctor's practices and procedures, but this disorder, which caused a tear in the lining of the main artery for blood leaving the heart, wasn't common and went largely undiagnosed.

It could be spotted with medical imaging equipment and could be treated, but if undiagnosed, it could be deadly.

If Nick were his pediatrician, or if he'd been on duty last night when the boy came in again, he would've automatically ordered the tests.

Not that he didn't trust Liam to follow through, but he made a mental note to make sure somebody followed up with the boy's doctor. He just didn't want to leave anything to chance.

He'd learned the hard way that sometimes if you looked away for just a moment you didn't get a second chance to make things right. Even if the tests came back negative, he'd rather rule out the deadly condition than have the boy suffer the consequences.

Even though Nick's full attention had been trained on Liam as they discussed the case, it didn't go unnoticed that Zane was at it again.

The guy was standing much too close to Becca. He had one arm braced against the wall as he leaned into her. He saw Becca take a step back and cross her arms as she angled her body away.

After Liam, armed with four freshly opened beers, went back into the living room to rejoin the guys and watch the last half of the game, Nick was better able to hear what Zane was saying to Becca.

The guy was asking her out again. Couldn't he read her body language? It didn't take a rocket scientist to see that she wasn't interested.

Obviously, the guy wasn't very good at picking up subtle clues. Nick went over and slid his arm around Becca's waist.

"Sorry, man, she's busy."

## Chapter Seven

"I'm not mad at you, Nick. I'm just confused because you keep sending me mixed messages. I get the feeling that you don't want a commitment—at least not a romantic commitment—but then when a man asks me to have dinner with him you tell him I'm busy?"

There. She'd said it. Now *almost everything* was out in the open. Except for the million-dollar question. She hoped he wouldn't make her spell it out. But on the drive back to her place from Liam and Kate's, she'd decided she was prepared to go for broke, because, really, what did she have to lose?

*Him, maybe?*

She didn't really have him. She was carrying his babies, and he seemed to be easing into the role of expectant father, but that didn't mean the two of them had a relationship beyond co-parenting.

"I'm sorry if I've been sending you mixed signals," he said as he steered the car into a visitors parking place in front of Becca's condo. "I guess I've been trying to figure this out myself. But spending time with you this week, and, yes, I'll admit, watching Zane make his big move, helped some things crystallize."

Becca's heart went all fluttery. Even though she knew she should tell Nick he couldn't have it both ways, when he turned to her and ran his thumb along her jawline, trailing it across her bottom lip, she met him halfway as he leaned in and covered her mouth with his.

His kiss was soft at first, transporting her to that magical place she always found herself in when she was with him.

He tasted vaguely of beer, but there was something else, something spicy and minty-cool freshening the taste. Something that tempted her to open her mouth wider and to lean in closer.

When she did, he deepened the kiss. Her whirling mind registered the velvety feel of his lips—those skilled, talented lips. God, he was just so darn good at this. So good at invading her personal space and instinctively knowing how to touch her just the way she wanted to be touched.

Becca didn't care about anything but this moment—this single moment suspended in time where nothing else mattered but the two of them and the babies growing inside of her.

"Should we go inside?" he asked, his breath whispering over her lips.

She answered him with another kiss before putting her hand on the door handle.

"Stay right there. I want to open your door for you."

"You're such a gentleman."

"I'm glad you think so, because the things I want to do to you might be considered ungentlemanly."

The thought took her breath away. "God, I hope so."

With that he let himself out of the car. The windows had begun to fog up. So she could see only the vague outline of him as he made his way around to her side.

She knew what this meant. She knew she was letting this happen again without any promises or pledges from him. And she thought of how well their bodies worked together, how he felt inside her, and that was all the promise she needed.

He helped her out of the car and put his arm around her, pulling her close and nibbling at her ear and her neck as they walked toward her front door.

"Do you know how crazy you are making me?" she asked as she took her keys out of her purse.

"How crazy? Tell me everything. How does this make you feel?"

As she unlocked the door, he positioned himself behind her, and she could feel his arousal through her coat. He moved her hair to one side to give himself better access to her neck, and the way he licked and trailed kisses made her stupid with lust.

His hands found their way inside her coat to her breasts; she inhaled sharply. If she couldn't open the door, they might just have to make love out here. He slipped his hands underneath her blouse and found her sensitive nipples. He knew just the right amount of pressure to make her want to cry out.

Thank God she was able to get the key in the lock and open the door. She pulled him inside and barely

had time to shut the door when he turned her around
and backed her up against the wall. She locked her
hands around his neck, and he ravished her with deep
kisses that blocked out everything else but him.

He slid his hands along her thigh, pausing at the
crook of her knee, and drew her leg up and around
him. He pushed his arousal into her, and she thrust
back.

"God, Becca. Who's making who crazy now?"

She dug her fingers into the hair on the back of his
head and pulled his mouth back to hers. He lifted her
up so that she could encircle him with both legs, and
they stayed like that kissing and thrusting, until she
pulled away and said, "Let's go into the bedroom."

Before he set her down, he looked into her eyes.
"Becca, I want to be here for you. I don't know if I'll
be very good at it—"

"But you are, Nick. I don't understand why you can't
see that."

"I have a history of messing things up when it comes
to family. I was married once before, but it didn't work
out, and then—"

He choked on his words, but he cleared his throat.

"I just don't have a very good track record when
it comes to family. Everything I touch seems to disintegrate."

"That's not true. You are a gifted doctor. You save
lives, Nick. That's sort of the opposite of making
things disintegrate."

He set her down gently and took a step back, rak-
ing his hair out of his eyes and looking more intense
than she'd ever seen him look.

"Do you want to talk about this?" she asked.

"Not really. Not now. Another time. But I want you to know that there is nobody else but you, and if you want to try to make this work, that's what I want, too."

She took him by the hand and led him into her bedroom, where they kissed softly, gently, for what seemed an eternity—or maybe it was only a moment. Time was suspended, until he picked her up and set her tenderly on the bed.

"I didn't realize you had a fireplace in here," he said. "I'll start a fire. I don't want you to get cold."

"Are you kidding? Here with you like this, there's no way I could get cold. Forget the fire."

He kissed her, and she felt it all the way to her toes. "Hold that thought. I'll be right back."

She watched him as he walked across the room and set logs and kindling on the fireplace's iron grate.

"There are matches on the mantel," she said. "In that little wooden box."

He picked up the matchbox and stared at it a moment before looking up at Becca.

"Are you sure this is okay? I mean, is it safe for the babies?"

"I talked to Dr. Stevens and he said it's fine. He said the only reason they classify my pregnancy *nearly normal* is because the uterus is really designed to only carry one baby. But since I'm healthy and everything seems to be fine, he said I should live as normal a life as possible within pregnancy parameters."

She was glad he asked, glad he cared about the well-being of their children. It made her want him all the more.

Minutes later the fire flared and spit tiny embers,

casting Nick in a warm glow of light and shadows. Everything about this man, from his tall, rugged build to his dark, brooding personality, set her senses on fire. The guy was a mystery, and she wanted to solve him, to get inside him and figure out what made him tick.

As he came back to her, he unbuttoned his shirt and let it fall to the floor. He unbuckled his belt and tossed it to the side. By the time he rejoined her on the bed, he was wearing only his pants.

Firelight danced across the taut muscles of his bare chest and shoulders. That's when she saw it—that single word tattooed on his left bicep in dark block letters.

*Ignosces.*

*Was that Latin?*

The first night they'd been together she hadn't noticed the date underneath the word: May 13, 1995.

"What's this?" She gently traced the word with her fingernail. "What does it mean?"

She felt him tense, maybe even pull away just a little, but she kept her hand on his arm.

He opened his mouth as if to speak but closed it before he could say a word. And then, as if thinking better of it, he said, "It means *forgive me.*"

Becca nodded, prepared to let it go at that, but he expounded.

"It's for my little brother. He died on May 13, 1995. He was only seven years old."

Becca's heart clenched. "I'm so sorry, Nick." She continued stroking his arm. "What happened?"

She knew it was a bad question to ask, even before his eyes darkened. She really wasn't trying to kill the mood. There was just so much between them that they needed to know about each other.

"That's a story for another day," he said.

Instinctively, she knew not to push him. It was the first personal detail—that and that he'd been married once before and he seemed to be convinced that everything worth loving fell apart in his hands. They were small steps. Tiny revelations she was learning about him. And if things kept going the way they were, she was confident that he would keep revealing himself to her bit by bit.

He swung his feet up onto the bed and propped himself up on one elbow. Reaching out, he smoothed a strand of hair off her forehead. His gaze was still dark, but now there was an intensity to it, and she felt herself melting like beeswax in his hands, especially when he trailed a thumb down her cheek, across her bottom lip, over the sensitive area at the base of her neck, until he reached the neckline of her sweater, where he teased the skin just below the surface.

Her mind skipped back to that first night they'd been together. He had instinctively known how to comfort her, how to please her. He'd made her feel as if she were the only woman in the world. Or at least the most adored woman in the world, and that's exactly how he was making her feel right now. Right now, in this moment, her world consisted of the two of them and the babies they'd already made. She couldn't imagine how life could be any sweeter.

His hands found their way to the bottom of her sweater and gently tugged it up and over her head, and then he made haste relieving her of her jeans, leaving her in just her bra and panties.

"Aren't you glad I stoked the fire?" he said through a lopsided smile that was more sexy than it was humorous.

"Yeah, you're good at that," she said, gazing up into his smoldering eyes. So many nights she'd thought of him, sure that she'd never see him again, never again feel his touch that seemed to instinctively know how to please her.

As if he could read her mind, his hands found her breasts, and he moved his thumb over her hard, sensitive nipple, which was aching for his touch. As he worked his magic, she found herself inhaling a ragged breath a second before a low moan escaped her lips. She didn't try to control her response; she let herself go, allowing her reaction to come spontaneously and unself-consciously.

She reached up and ran her hands over those shoulders that drove her crazy. His skin was as hot and his muscles as hard as a sheet of pressed steel. His body was smooth and strong with animal-like sexiness that had her summoning every ounce of self-control to keep from demanding that he take her right then and there. They were going to make love.

The heady realization racked Becca's body with shudders. She couldn't wait for him to do more of the same he'd done to her that first night they'd been together.

Of course, that night their lovemaking had created a baby—two babies. Right now, that seemed terribly romantic. Lying here with him naked and vulnerable, allowing him inside, past her personal barriers, there was no place to hide in the soft firelight. And that was fine because she couldn't recall ever wanting anything more.

He ran his hand down her thighs, sliding them all the way to her knees and then back up until his fingertips found their way inside the edge of her panties. Gently hooking his thumbs in the elastic, he tugged them down and slipped them off. Then he lifted her ever so slightly and removed her bra with a couple of deft movements.

It wasn't her lack of clothing that gave her pause as much as it was her emotional vulnerability. Could he read the desire in her eyes as clearly as she could read it in his? He put her at ease when he began placing gentle, unanticipated kisses on her body—on her forehead, on that ticklish spot behind her ears, trailing his way down until he'd reached the sensitive insides of her thighs.

Then he stopped, looking at her with possessive eyes. "I said I wanted to get to know you better." His voice was low and sexy. "Show me what I need to know."

He started running his hands over her, then he took her hand and moved it with his, allowing her to introduce him to her body, having her show him what she liked. This was something she'd never done during lovemaking.

He was incredibly gentle and generous. Not only did he know how to please, he seemed to give his all to every experience. Or maybe the explosiveness of his touch was a by-product of their personal chemistry.

Whatever the case, she loved everything he did. Everything he said. Everywhere he touched.

And then his tongue found its way to her center,

and he worked his magic until she cried out in pleasure that was so intense it radiated off her in waves.
Her first climax was compliments of his clever, teasing mouth, and the second time it was thanks to the
long, soft gliding strokes of his fingers.

Spellbound, she turned onto her side and braced
her hands on his strong, muscled chest, letting her
hands discover him, feeling every muscled ridge.
Then when she freed him of his pants and underwear
and took him into her hands, his head dropped back.

He groaned as she savored the hot, smooth length
of him.

Lowering her head, she swirled her tongue over
him. His whole body stiffened, and he let out a sound
that heartened and aroused her even more. With him,
she wanted to do things she'd never done before, had
never wanted to do with anyone else. She wanted him
to see her pleasure in doing them with him.

He must've known, because everything about him
was hard with arousal. And yet his hands were gentle
as he turned her over onto her back and stared lov-
ingly into her eyes.

"If you keep doing that, I won't be any good to
you. We have a lot more territory to cover."

He leaned down and kissed her softly and slowly.
"Becca, I've never seen anything more perfect than
you in my life," he said as he positioned himself over
her. "You are flawless."

His words nearly brought her to tears. No one had
ever called her flawless. No one had even remotely
thought of her that way. Or at least they hadn't told
her if they had. She'd spent so much time trying to

live up to everyone's expectations—the couple of former lovers she'd had, her family...

"You don't know how many nights I've lain awake, thinking about this moment when we would be together again like this."

She wanted to tell him that she felt the same way, but she was afraid that if she spoke she might break the spell or, even worse, wake up from this lovely dream.

Then he finally thrust into her, filling her with his muscle and heat. She gripped his shoulders tight, matching him thrust for thrust until she exploded in an orgasm that seemed to last forever.

His forehead glistened with sweat and his biceps bulged. Their gazes locked and he built a strong rhythm that got faster and faster until his teeth clenched and his face contorted. A long, guttural growl emanated from his throat. Then very slowly, ever so tenderly, he lowered his body to cover hers.

As a general rule, Nick wasn't a fan of shopping malls, but over coffee and bagels early Monday morning before they both went to work, somehow Becca had talked him into meeting her at the mall after he got off work at seven that evening.

She wanted to look at baby furniture in Dallas. After last night, she might be able to talk him into just about anything.

He had taken a risk making love to her again—crossing that line and making implied promises he still, in his moments of doubt, wasn't sure he could keep.

But damn, they were good together. In bed, they

had a chemistry that could scorch the sun. He just hoped it didn't mean that the relationship was combustible in other ways. Even that possibility didn't burn away the reality that he liked waking up beside her.

His other reason for meeting her at the mall was that he wanted to talk to her about Dr. Stevens's caution that, because they were pregnant with twins, the pregnancy was considered *nearly normal.*

Becca was healthy and Stevens had said sex was okay, but during a slow moment at work, Nick had done some research and discovered that even the slightly elevated risk associated with carrying twins warranted extra precautions as the pregnancy progressed.

He'd also picked out the best hospital in the area that specialized in high-risk births. He'd been eager to talk to her about it because he wanted her to tour the hospital to make sure she was comfortable with it, but he didn't want to alarm her any more than Dr. Stevens had. Just as he started to broach the subject, a woman who was modeling a ruby ring and necklace at the entrance to a jewelry store spoke to Becca.

"This would look lovely on you," she said, "with your fair skin and dark hair."

Becca stopped to admire the jewelry.

"Would you like to try it on?" the woman asked.

"Oh, no, that's okay," Becca said as she continued to admire the necklace. "We're in a hurry today. Maybe another time."

The way she lingered over the unusual piece belied her objections.

Nick looked at his watch. "Go ahead," he urged. "We have a few minutes."

"We still need to look at furniture," Becca said. "I know you're tired after working. I'd planned on making this quick."

"We're fine."

Becca smiled and followed the saleswoman into the store.

Once inside, the woman unhooked the ruby-studded gold chain from her neck and slipped it around Becca's neck.

"Doesn't she look exquisite wearing the necklace?"

The woman was an excellent salesperson. She was definitely working hard to earn her commission.

"She is exquisite even without the necklace," he said.

He smiled as he watched Becca's cheeks turn a pretty shade of pink. It reminded him of how color had touched her features last night as he'd made love to her in the firelight.

"Try on the ring, too." The woman took it off her finger and handed it to Becca.

"Historically, rubies have been associated with passion. They're also a symbol of romance and adventure. So, Romeo, this is a nice gift to get your sweetheart."

Yes, she was definitely working it. He had to admire her tenacity.

"Do you want the necklace?" he asked. "I'd like for you to have it."

"Oh, no, Nick, I couldn't. I mean, it's gorgeous, but it's far too expensive. I was just trying it on for fun."

Apologetically, she turned to the saleswoman. "I didn't mean to waste your time."

The woman smiled at her. "No apology needed. We're slow right now, anyway. I'm happy you tried it on."

As Becca took one last wistful glance in the mirror, the woman slipped Nick her card and mouthed, *For Christmas?*

Nick nodded. It would be a good present, he thought as he tucked the card into his pocket.

As they walked away from the store, Becca said, "I'm sorry that woman put you in an awkward position. It was sweet of you to offer to get me the necklace. But you didn't have to."

"One thing you definitely need to know about me is that it's not easy to coerce me into anything I don't want to do. I wouldn't have offered if I'd felt pressured."

"Good to know," Becca said, and a sensuous light passed between them.

He hated to potentially kill the mood. "There's something I need to talk to you about."

"Should I be worried?"

"No," he said as they entered the department store. "In fact, it should be something to ease your mind."

She slanted him a dubious look. "Okay. Why is that not comforting?"

"You haven't even heard what I have to say." They got on the escalator to the second floor, where apparently they kept the baby furniture. This was foreign territory. "After Dr. Stevens mentioned that a twin pregnancy was considered slightly high risk, I did some research."

He told her about the hospital in Dallas that specialized in high-risk births.

She frowned but didn't say anything.

"Think about it," he said. "Your obstetrician is in Dallas, and you work there. You're there almost as much as you're in Celebration. So, really, it only makes sense."

They stepped off the escalator and followed the signs to the baby department.

"What if I go into labor in the middle of the night? It would be just my luck."

"You can call me and I'll come and get you."

"I don't know if it makes sense, since Celebration Memorial is five minutes from my condo. I'm having twins, not brain surgery. I'm healthy. Do we really need to make the twenty-minute drive?"

She pointed at a crib that was adorned with a yellow checked blanket turned down over yellow flannel sheets. "What do you think? Natural wood or white for the furniture?"

"Whatever you want," he said. "Will you just agree to go for the tour? The hospital set it up for me as a professional courtesy."

"I'll think about it."

"Fair enough. The appointment isn't until December 9, but that'll be here sooner than you think."

"Becca?"

They both turned at a woman's voice behind them. Nick watched all the color drain out of Becca's cheeks when she saw her sister, Rosanna.

"What are you doing here? Are you looking at baby furniture?"

"Rosanna, hi. No, we are shopping for a baby gift."

"Oh, really? From my angle it looked like you were looking at furniture."

"Sorry to disappoint you, but we aren't." The clipped tone Becca used with her sister was foreign and far from the sweet, gentle nature that he'd come to know.

"Who's pregnant?" Rosanna was openly eyeing Becca's stomach.

"Nobody you know. Rosanna, you remember Nick, don't you?"

"Of course, the football game Friday night. Good to see you again. I have to run. If you do find yourself in the market for baby furniture, don't forget I still have Victor's stuff. It's in the attic at Mom and Dad's. I'm sure they'd be happy to get it down for you."

Becca smiled at her sister, but there was an obvious lack of warmth. "I'll keep that in mind. For future reference. See you later."

Rosanna walked in one direction. Becca and Nick headed toward the exit.

As soon as she was sure Rosanna was out of earshot, Becca turned to Nick. "What was that? Of all the people to run into right now, right here? Why her? It's as if she has radar that helps her zero in on finding me at my weakest." She put a hand on Nick's arm as if she needed to steady herself. He put his arm around her as they walked.

"Nick, I have to tell my parents. If they end up hearing the news from someone else first, they'll never forgive me. It's already going to be hard enough when they hear it from me. I just need to do it."

He reached out and took her hand. "I'll go with

you. It's all in how you present it. If you act like there's something wrong, then they'll take it badly. If we present it like the good news that it is, they'll have to be happy for us."

She scoffed and picked up a tiny pink outfit. "Obviously, you don't know my parents."

"Please, don't take this wrong, but how old are you?"

Her brows furrowed. "We're having twins, and you don't even know how old I am. We are doing things backward, aren't we?"

"We are two adults, and we are playing the cards that we've been dealt."

She gave him a one-shoulder shrug. "I guess you're right. And for the record, I'm twenty-five."

"You are a grown woman. You have your own home. You're supporting yourself. I know this will sound harsh, but your parents shouldn't get to set the rules in this circumstance."

She nodded, but she looked as if she was trying to convince herself that was true. "Do you really want to go with me? Because you don't have to."

"Of course I will. I—" A foreign feeling, that for a fleeting moment felt something like love, whooshed through him. He took a deep breath and realized it was just the protectiveness and an odd sort of possessiveness he felt for Becca. "We're in this together. Come on. I'll walk you to your car."

They'd come in separate cars, since he was meeting her after work.

Out in the parking lot, Becca said, "Before you make up your mind about going with me, I have to warn you. My parents will insist that we get married."

"That's not their decision to make."

"You're right. But they'll insist. So just be prepared. They like to pretend that they're terribly old-fashioned, but really they're just holier than thou. What's ironic is they've both been unhappy in their own marriage for as far back as I can remember. They've done a very good job of pretending and putting up a front so that everyone else thinks they have this idealistic life. They've always held themselves a little above everyone else, which I believe is just a defense mechanism. Rosanna got pregnant with Victor when she was fifteen. She was always the wild child and I was the good girl. My parents pretended to be the happy couple. I guess we all just fell into those roles. My parents—it's going to kill them to know that both of their daughters got pregnant outside of marriage."

More pieces of the Becca puzzle, and they explained a lot. She was the good girl of the family who had probably jumped through hoops all of her life in order to win her parents' approval. Rosanna was the one who pretended not to give a damn about what anyone thought. Nick knew how that was, pretending not to care. Pretty soon, it became a way of life. If you grew a tough hide, no one could hurt you. But to keep people from hurting you, you had to stop letting people in, and pretty soon people just stopped trying to reach you.

"Is Victor's father involved?"

Becca shook her head. "He hasn't been around at all. Victor has never met him."

"Well, therein lies one huge difference. I plan to

be there for you and our children. Tell me when you need me, and I'll make sure I'm there."

"I'll see if they're available tomorrow evening."

## Chapter Eight

"You're what?" Isabel Flannigan shrieked.

"Nick and I are pregnant with twins," Becca repeated.

"And you're getting married, Rebecca."

It was a command, not a question. And it tightened every fiber in Becca's body.

"No, we have no plans to get married, Mom."

She glanced at her father, who was sitting quietly in the striped gondola chair with his arms crossed. He was staring somewhere into the distance, and he hadn't said a word since Becca had broken the news.

"I will be there for Becca and the babies," Nick said. "They will have my full emotional and financial support."

Isabel glared at Nick.

"And are we supposed to cheer for you for owning up to your mistake?"

"Mom. These are your grandchildren. Please, don't

call them a mistake. They may have been unplanned, but they are certainly not a mistake."

Isabel continued her tirade as if she hadn't heard a word Becca had said after *Nick and I are pregnant with twins*. "Getting married is only the decent thing to do. You play, you pay, Rebecca."

Becca wanted to tell her mother that the reason she wasn't getting married was because Nick didn't love her. Not that way. But her biggest fear was being shoehorned into a loveless marriage, and because of it, she and her children and her coerced husband would end up living an unhappy life.

*Just like you, Mom and Dad.*

But of course she didn't say that. If she had, she would've said it in front of Nick, and the wrath she would've had to endure for embarrassing her mother in front of a stranger would've made the admonishment she'd received after breaking the news of the pregnancy look like nothing.

"With all due respect, Mrs. Flannigan, we didn't come to ask for your advice or your blessing."

*Oh, good Lord.* All the air whooshed out of Becca's lungs. And she wanted to hug Nick for it. He'd just succeeded in very politely and respectfully putting Isabel Flannigan in her place. How in the world had he managed that?

Oh, but wait, he wasn't finished.

"Mr. and Mrs. Flannigan, Becca and I are here out of courtesy to you. You're the grandparents of our children, and I hope that we can count on you to be supportive, but we need to establish that the way Becca and I choose to live our lives and how we raise our children is our decision."

Isabel opened her mouth as if she were going to say something but decided better. That was a first.

"Of course it's your decision," said Patrick Flannigan. It was the first indication that he'd heard a single word spoken this evening. "I just hope you understand this comes as a shock. It's the last thing we expected from Rebecca. We always thought she would take a more traditional path. And, young man, we met you for the first time five days ago. We don't know anything about you. So why don't we start with…how long have you known our daughter?"

Nick and Rebecca looked at each other. *If ever there was a chance that he could read her mind, please, let it be now.* Surely he would know that they didn't need to know about the one-night stand. But just in case—

"We met at the hospital, the night of Victor's accident."

"Let the man speak for himself, Rebecca," her mother said.

She hated how a single comment from her mother could make her feel fourteen years old. She braced herself for her parents to do the math and, from the sum of the equation, figure out she'd gotten pregnant that night.

Instead, her mother insisted, "Why were you at the hospital the night of Victor's accident?"

"I'm an emergency medicine doctor," Nick said. "Becca had some questions about her nephew's condition, and I was happy to answer them. We had dinner, and the rest is history."

*Yes. Perfect.* Becca held her breath for a moment,

waiting for them to catch on, but if they knew, they didn't mention it.

*Thank you.* Becca glanced at Nick again and there was that subtle, sensual bond that connected them like a thread.

He understood her. At that moment she thought she might possibly be in love for the first time in her life.

After Isabel and Patrick Flannigan were satisfied with the grilling that they had given Nick, Isabel said, "Then I suppose you and Rebecca will be doing double duty on Thanksgiving. I'm sure you want to see your parents, too."

As much as Becca hated to admit it, it was a good question. Nick always seemed to skirt the issue when family came up. She was curious to know more about his folks. She knew his younger brother had passed away much too early, but she had no idea if he had other siblings.

"My mother is no longer living," Nick said in a very matter-of-fact tone. "My father lives in Florida. So, no, I won't see him for Thanksgiving."

"Did you invite him for the holiday?"

"I'm sure he has to work."

"Couldn't he make time?"

"Mom, really? Don't you think you've interrogated Nick enough for tonight?"

Isabel pinned Becca with a withering glare. "Rebecca, this man is the father of our grandchildren. I don't think it's out of line to ask a few questions to get to know him.

"Have you broken the news about the twins to him yet?" she pressed.

"No, not yet. We wanted to share it with you and Mr. Flannigan first."

*Ooh! Brownie points. Nice touch, Nick.*

To Becca's surprise, Isabel's face softened.

"Since you have no family in town, we will set a place for you at our table."

Becca blinked. Nick didn't know this, but this was a huge gesture on her mother's part. She guarded her holidays zealously. They were for family only. In fact, her brother Mark's wife, Beth, had not been invited until after she and Mark were engaged. It seemed that Nick had managed to skip a couple of steps. Or maybe babies trumped marriage? Who knew what logic Isabel applied.

"That's a very gracious offer," Nick said. "But I'm scheduled to work Thursday."

The silence was deafening.

"But I'm scheduled for the early shift this week. How about if I come over after I get off work?"

"Nick, you'll be exhausted. Mom, he works twelve-hour shifts. I'm sure he doesn't want to come after work."

"Don't be ridiculous, Rebecca. It's Thanksgiving. It's when families get together. And it will be as good a time as any for the two of you to announce the pregnancy and any other plans you might come up with between now and then."

Tuesday evening after leaving her parents' house, Becca was certain of two things: first, Nick had managed the impossible—he had basically charmed her mother into submission—and second, she was falling in love with Nick. He'd walked that fine line between saying the right things and not kowtowing.

Since Nick had agreed to endure Thanksgiving Flannigan-style, she'd given him some space Wednesday night. He had to work the 7:00 a.m. to 7:00 p.m. shift. He was sure to be exhausted.

But Becca would've been lying to herself if she didn't admit she'd been a little disappointed when he hadn't called last night. Of course, she hadn't called him, either—hence the giving him space part. But it was the first day that had gone by since they'd received the results of the pregnancy test that they hadn't at least texted.

On Thursday morning, she picked up her phone, brought up his number and sent him a message:

Happy Thanksgiving! Looking forward to seeing you tonight.

She stared at the screen expectantly for a moment, tamping down the hope that he would text her right back.

But he didn't.

She swallowed her disappointment. He was working. He'd been there since before she'd even gotten out of bed. She needed to cut him some slack.

Mandatory family dinners were never easy to get through. They usually involved at least thirty relatives. Of course, there were her mother's judgmental comments and her sister's temperamental prickliness. Someone always had too much to drink and ended up saying or doing something that offended someone else.

For the most part, it was like a three-ring circus.

Her aunts and uncles were generally pleasant, for the most part. Mark and Beth were nice and Becca tried to stick with them or at least fly under the radar until she'd helped wash, dry and put away the last dish, and she could take her leave until the next time.

What was it like to be part of a family that wasn't quite so dysfunctional?

As she took the pumpkin pies she'd prepared from scratch out of the oven, she vowed when her daughters were born she would do everything in her power to foster a good relationship with them. Daughters? Well, that was a Freudian slip if she'd ever heard one. She had no idea what the sex of her babies would be— if they were fraternal or identical—and, yes, when it came right down to it, she simply wanted healthy children, whatever the sex. Still, deep inside she knew she'd love to have a couple of little girls with whom she could have a good relationship and do all of the things she wished she and her mother could have done and shared.

How had her relationship with her mother ended up getting so off track? All she had ever done was try to please her mother, try to make her see that she was worthy of her love. In all fairness, her mother loved her in her own quirky way. But she always seemed to disapprove. It was her mother's approval she'd always been trying to earn. No matter what she did or how hard she tried, she never seemed to measure up.

As Becca carried the trays with her homemade pies to her car, she vowed to never make her children feel as if they had to earn her approval.

The first thing her mother said to her when she

arrived at the house at four o'clock was "You're late, Rebecca."

"It's four o'clock, mother. We won't serve dinner until seven-thirty."

"Well, since I gave the staff Thanksgiving Day off, it would've been nice for you to offer to help."

Of course, she was being sarcastic. She didn't have staff. Isabel Flannigan prided herself on being a homemaker—and a darn good one at that, if you were giving credit where credit was due. Besides, she probably wouldn't have been able to find somebody to measure up to her standards if she could have had staff. And then there was the problem of finding someone who actually had the hide of steel to withstand her mother's scrutiny on an hourly basis. Becca couldn't even imagine such a person existed.

"Why didn't you ask me to come earlier? I'm not very good at reading minds. Where is Rosanna? Is she here yet?"

"Oh, heavens, no. I want this to be a pleasant day. She and I would simply be at each other's throats. I told her and Victor to arrive around six o'clock."

So that was the secret, huh? If you made Isabel miserable enough, you were released from family obligation. Her sister was smarter than her mother gave her credit for.

"Well, then, she gets to do the cleanup," Becca said. "Just because she's hard to get along with doesn't mean she gets a vacation."

"Oh, Rebecca, stop saying nasty things about your sister. Do you hear yourself?"

*No, Mom, I can't seem to hear myself over the echo of your negativity.*

That's what Rosanna would have said, and the two of them would've gotten into a sparring match that would've lasted until Rosanna left in tears or their mother ended up going upstairs with a *sick headache*. Becca, on the other hand, swallowed her words, sat down at the kitchen table and started peeling the sweet potatoes.

She'd rather cook than clean up, anyway. And with Nick here, she'd have a good reason to leave the cleanup to Rosanna. Becca's stomach gave a nervous turn when she remembered running into Rosanna at the mall. Of course, there was the little matter of the little white lie she'd told when Rosanna had been quizzing her about why she was browsing in the baby department. There would be hell to pay for that one.

For a moment Becca contemplated pulling Rosanna aside and sharing the news with her before she and Nick told the rest of the family. But as quickly as the idea presented itself, Becca decided against it. She wanted to keep today as uncomplicated as possible. Despite how her parents had mandated that she and Nick announce their news to the rest of the family today, they were onboard with it. It made sense. The next time the entire family would be together would be Christmas.

She wanted to share the news with her friends. Since Celebration was such a small town, if she did that, a family member was bound to find out. She wouldn't want to receive news like that secondhand. So this was a do unto others as she would hope that they would do for her sort of decision. But Rosanna could be such a loose cannon, if Becca tried to appease her, she might end up spilling the beans before

Becca and Nick had a chance to make the announcement. Faced with the potential fallout of that and her sister's inevitable protests that Becca had lied to her, Becca was better prepared to deal with Rosanna.

All she had to say to her sister about that day at the mall was she didn't want to tell her about the babies until she and Nick had told Mom and Dad.

Becca was surprised how fast time flew. She'd been busy in the kitchen all afternoon—even if her mother had insisted that she stay seated. It was amazing what could be accomplished at the kitchen table. Now it was seven-fifteen, and Victor had been enlisted by his grandmother to round up the crew and instruct them to wash their hands and be at their respective places at the table—there were place cards for the assigned seating, and Victor had a list and was to help them find their way. His chest was puffed out with the importance of this job that allowed him to tell the adults what to do, for a change, rather than being bossed by the adults.

As her mother placed the turkey on the serving tray, Becca was anxiously aware that Nick had not yet arrived.

An unsettled wave of apprehension washed over her. What if he'd changed his mind? What if he wasn't coming?

That was a ridiculous thought. Had Nick let her down yet?

No. But after Tuesday night's interrogation, she really wouldn't blame him if he decided to skip the Flannigan's annual turkey brawl.

*Come on, Becca. Buck up. He had to work until seven. Maybe something came up.*

Like a better offer.

No. That was decidedly not the man she'd fallen in love with. He'd been her rock, her touchstone. While she knew she was capable of breaking the news of the pregnancy to her family, she had liked the idea of him standing beside her, helping her set the tone, when they made the announcement.

As the parade of side dishes, dinner rolls and condiments started to roll toward the table, Becca slipped off to check her phone. Just in case.

Her heart nearly stopped when she saw the text from Nick.

Sorry for the late notice. I have an emergency and I can't get away from the hospital. Will try to stop by later if it's not too late. Please give your parents my regrets. Happy Thanksgiving.

## Chapter Nine

Nick steered his car onto the Flannigans' paved circular driveway and parked behind a dark Toyota Prius.

After work, he'd gone home to take a quick shower and trade his scrubs for a pair of black pants and a button-down. He swapped out the Harley for the Jeep before going to Thanksgiving dinner. He'd done it for Becca's sake more than anything. After meeting Isabel and Patrick and informing them that their daughter was having his babies, he'd come away with the impression that they'd like him even less if he showed up on a bike.

He wasn't trying to impress them or win them over. Her mother had already proven she could be a handful, and Nick simply didn't want to add fuel to the fire.

That was all right. He was in a good mood. He always was after he saved someone's life.

He grabbed the bottle of merlot he'd bought for the occasion and headed up the porch steps that led to the front door of the two-story brick home.

This was the home where Becca had grown up.

Before he reached the porch, he wondered which window had been hers and how many boys might have stood below it and tossed pebbles to get her attention.

The gas coach lamps glowed, and other ambient lighting lit up the lush, well-landscaped yard that still looked remarkably green despite the unseasonably cold temperatures. The redbrick Colonial wasn't a mansion by any means, but it certainly wasn't a shack.

It was a nice upper-middle class abode that any family would be lucky to call home. It was a far cry from the places he'd lived as a child as he'd shuffled back and forth between his parents' places. They were usually leased apartments in a part of town where rent was *affordable*. His parents' divorce had not only torn apart the family, but it had also ruined both of them financially.

On the porch, Nick could see through the illuminated windows into the dining room, where a crowd was gathered around the table enjoying dessert.

Maybe he should've texted Becca before he came, but he was already so late that he'd been in a hurry to get there. Now it seemed pointless to text from the front porch.

He rang the doorbell and heard the sound of running feet and a couple *I'll get its*—a herd of children, no doubt, racing to answer the door.

He was right. When the door opened, a small crowd of kids clustered around the threshold.

"Who are you?" asked a boy who may have been six or seven years old. His nose was covered with freckles, and he was missing his two front teeth.

Nick shifted his weight from one foot to the other. "I'm Nick. Who are you?"

"My mom says I can't talk to strangers," said the boy, who was obviously the spokesperson for the munchkins.

"Probably a good idea," Nick said. "Would you please go get Becca so I can talk to her?"

"He's here to see Becca?" a little blonde girl asked. "How come he's not at his house having Thanksgiving?"

"Because he's here to see Becca," the freckle-faced boy said, in that way older and usually self-designated wiser kids talked down to younger kids.

"He's right," Nick said. "I'm supposed to come over and have Thanksgiving with Becca. Right here in this house with you."

The little girl ducked back behind the door.

The freckled kid assessed him for a moment before bellowing, *"Beccaaaaa!"*

He drew out the *aaaaa* until a startled-looking Becca came to the door.

"Oh! Nick. It's you." Her face brightened. "You're here. How long have you been standing there?"

"Not long. They were just telling me that they're not allowed to talk to strangers."

Becca laughed. "Right. Well, uh, thanks, Jesse. This is Nick. He's my friend. It's okay to invite him in."

Becca ruffled the kid's sandy-brown hair.

"You can come in," Jesse said, stepping back. "But I don't think we have any turkey left. We have Brussels sprouts, though."

"What are you talking about, Jesse? We still have some turkey."

As Nick stepped into the foyer, the kid frowned at Becca and then put his finger to his lips and made a shushing noise. "I'm taking that home. Auntie Bel said I could take it home. He can have the *Brussels sprouts.*"

"Jesse, you need to share. Nick just got off work, and I'm sure he's hungry. Believe me, there will be plenty of turkey for you and everyone else to take home if Nick has some. It's cold outside. Please, move out of the way so he can come in."

Either Jesse was easily convinced or he lost interest, because the next thing Nick knew the boy and his wolf pack had run off, leaving him gloriously alone in the foyer with Becca.

"Hi," he said, leaning in a little bit.

"Hi," she repeated, meeting him halfway. "I'm glad to see you."

He kissed her, and suddenly her lips were the only thing in the world he craved. He was lost in the taste of her cranberry-and-spice lips until he heard giggles coming from around the corner.

"See!" Jesse said victoriously. "I told you if we left they'd kiss." This was uproariously funny to the brood, who were holding their stomachs and throwing back their small heads in laughter. Then when Jesse started chanting, *"Kissing! Kissing!"* his band of mini minions began following him around the house reciting in unison.

"That's embarrassing. Sorry. Welcome to Thanksgiving with the Flannigans. You can run now and save yourself."

"That's all right. I'm up for it."

Becca leaned in and planted one more kiss on his lips. "Come on in, but don't say I didn't warn you."

Of course, the house looked the same, but it had a decidedly different air with all the rooms lit up and the sound of people chatting and laughing. Good smells filled the air, and Nick's stomach rumbled in appreciation.

Becca paused outside the dining room. "I was afraid you wouldn't be able to make it."

"I'm sorry about that," he said. "We had an emergency. This boy who was in the ER twice before with chest pains was back today."

Becca grimaced. "Poor kid. And on Thanksgiving, too."

"I confirmed a diagnosis of aortic dissection. He had a tear in the lining of the main artery for blood leaving the heart. If we hadn't caught it, he could've died."

"Nick. You saved his life."

He gave a quick nod. "Do you think that earns me a beer?"

Becca gave him a hug and then looked up at him. "You can have whatever you want."

He liked the way she felt in his arms. It felt like coming home. Or he imagined it did. It was unlike any home he'd ever known.

A large man with a red face turned the corner of the dining room and nearly ran into them. "Hey, you two. Knock that off. No wonder the kids are running around here chanting about kissing."

His tone suggested he was joking. Nonetheless, Nick stepped away from Becca.

"Uncle Don," Becca said. "I want you to meet Nick Ciotti. Nick, this is my uncle Don."

Nick shook the man's hand. "Is this the boyfriend your mother was telling us about?" Don said.

Becca sputtered a bit. "You know how Mom is."

"She mentioned that there might be wedding bells in the future. She's a good catch, man. Don't let her get away."

Nick wasn't quite sure what to say. So he simply nodded in what he hoped was a noncommittal way.

The collar of his shirt suddenly felt tight, despite the fact that it was open. It was a little warm in the house, despite the nearly freezing temperatures outside.

He was probably coming down off the adrenaline rush brought on by the fast pace of the day. Plus, he was hungry, and he really could use that beer.

"Uncle Don, Nick was just telling me he saved a boy's life today. He's an ER doctor at the hospital, and he's just coming from work."

Becca definitely had a talent for steering an uncomfortable conversation in a different direction.

"Is that so? Well, it'll be good to have a doctor in the family. Good job, Becs. I need to run in *here* for a minute." He gestured toward a room off the hallway that led to the living room. "I'll catch up with you lovebirds a little later."

After Don disappeared, Becca made an exasperated face at Nick. "I warned you."

"And that you did." He hadn't expected so much

pressure. He hoped her family wouldn't turn into an angry mob after they broke the news about the pregnancy.

He was about to ask her if she really thought tonight was a good night to tell them and suggest that maybe they should do it in smaller groups, when Isabel found them.

"Nick, how lovely to see you." She leaned in and offered her cheek. "I was afraid you wouldn't be able to join us."

"I'm sorry I'm late, Mrs. Flannigan. I got tied up at work."

Isabel cocked her head to the right, but her posture was still impeccable. "Nothing serious, I hope."

As Don passed by again, he said, "He saved a kid's life tonight."

Isabel's eyes flew open wide. "You did? And on Thanksgiving. Oh, Nick, I'll bet the family is so very thankful for you today. We have a hero, right here in our midst."

Nick waved her off and tried to tell her it was nothing, really. "It was all in a day's work."

But Isabel wasn't listening. She was already leading the way into the dining room, where at least twenty people were crowded around the large formal table talking and eating. A cornucopia resided at the center of the table. Along the back wall was an ornate wooden buffet that housed a fancy silver coffee service, complete with creamer and sugar bowl situated on a large, gleaming tray. At least a half dozen pies of various types were positioned on either side.

"Please, come into the dining room and sit down. Victor, move so Nick can sit down and eat." The skinny teenage boy cast a moody glance over his left shoulder, but he obediently got up from the table.

"Sit down right there, Nick. Becca will bring you a place setting and fix you a plate."

"Really, I don't want to put you out. If you've already put the food away, I'll just have a beer or coffee. Or whatever you have handy."

"Nonsense. It's Thanksgiving. On Thanksgiving you will eat turkey and all the trimmings. Now, sit down. Becca, don't just stand there. Go get his food."

Nick slanted Becca a glance, worried that she might be bristling over her mother's directives. But she didn't seem bothered. She was already on her way out of the room.

He could see others through the doorway that led to the kitchen and still more people sitting in the living room, where Nick and Becca had sat with Isabel and Patrick two nights ago.

After Nick's mom had died, it was just him and his dad. Caiden was gone, and his dad wasn't close with his extended family. There had been no holidays with grandparents or aunts, uncles and cousins.

A gathering of the boisterous Flannigan clan was a little overwhelming. To say the least.

Especially when Don said in his booming voice, "Hey, everyone, this is Nick, Becca's boyfriend. He saved a kid's life tonight. That's why he's late to Thanksgiving."

Sounds of awed admiration echoed through the room. Things like this were bright spots, but they really were just part of a day's work. He forgot how it must sound when civilians heard about lives being saved. Especially when they were young.

As he waited for Becca to return, he fielded questions about the procedure. He was careful to keep the details general enough so as not to violate the boy's privacy. But then again, as cool as people who weren't in the business may have thought hospital talk was, it didn't take long before the average person's eyes started glazing over.

Soon enough, most everyone returned to their own conversations. A few talked to Nick, asking him about himself and how he and Becca met and how long they'd been dating. Until finally Becca presented Nick with a frosty mug of beer and a heaping plate of food.

He'd barely finished his meal when Patrick entered the room. "Nick, you're here."

He offered his hand, and Nick stood before he shook it.

"You might as well remain standing," Patrick instructed him. "Now is as good a time as any to share your news with the family. People are going to start leaving pretty soon, and we don't want anyone left out."

As Isabel herded the others into the dining room or at least within earshot, Nick glanced around the table.

Working in the emergency room, he was used to dealing with blood and guts and some of the strangest and typically scary things a layperson could imagine. Nothing much fazed him.

Except for the Flannigans.

He found the lot of them terrifying.

This was some serious family togetherness. They were a unit. A clan. They were in each other's business, and the elders definitely ran the show, dictating when everyone should jump and exactly how high.

Comparatively, Nick was a lone wolf. He preferred to ride a motorcycle, and no one gave him the hairy eyeball. If he wanted a tattoo, he didn't need to ask permission. If he chose to, he could eat a plateful of candy corn for his Thanksgiving dinner. Although, he had to admit that the dinner was delicious. It was perfect. Like a Norman Rockwell scene or a cover of the *Saturday Evening Post*.

Now it was suddenly crystal clear why Becca had hesitated to tell her family about the pregnancy. He wasn't so sure he wanted to announce this rather personal piece of news to the family.

"Is everyone here?" Isabel hollered. "Nick and Becca have an announcement for the entire family."

"You're getting married, aren't you?" Don said. "I knew it. I called it."

"No, Uncle Don," Becca said. "We're going to have a baby. Twins, actually."

Virtual crickets chirped in the dining room.

Everyone had been stunned.

Stunned silent.

Becca couldn't remember this ever happening. Not even when Rosanna had gotten pregnant. Of course, Becca had been eleven years old at the time and she couldn't recall her parents making such a cavalier announcement. But she figured everyone would know sooner or later. At least this way they seemed supportive.

Becca tried to avoid looking at Rosanna, but guilt must've made her glance over. Her sister was sitting there with a smug smirk on her face. Becca was holding her breath, hoping against hope that Rosanna would not bring up running into her and Nick in the baby department.

Aunt Millie was the first to speak. "So this means you're getting married, right?"

Becca could feel Nick withdrawing under all the pressure.

"Actually, we have no plans for that, right now."

It surprised Becca how much it hurt to say those words, more than she'd expected. And she had to admit that she was disappointed when Nick didn't speak up and say something that vaguely hinted that marriage wasn't out of the question.

Just because she was falling in love with him didn't mean the feeling was mutual. And the only thing worse than not being married to the father of your child was to be married to a man who didn't love you.

One person could not bring all the love to a marriage. She'd learned that through her parents.

"We're working on that," Isabel said without a trace of teasing in her tone. "We'll have them walking down the aisle before next Thanksgiving. Just watch."

Obviously, she wasn't joking. Becca wanted to melt into a puddle and disappear through the fine cracks in the mahogany floorboards.

Suddenly, Nick stood. "It's nice to meet you," he said to no one in particular. "Thank you for letting me share your Thanksgiving, but I really should be going."

"You haven't had your pie yet," said Aunt Millie.

Nick smiled at her, but Becca could see the weariness in his eyes and around the corners of his mouth. "Everything was so delicious, I'm stuffed. I couldn't eat another bite, but thank you."

Meeting the entire family like this, under these circumstances, had been a lot to swallow. She didn't blame him for wanting to leave.

"Get yourself a piece to take home with you," Aunt Mille said. "Your bride-to-be made all those pies. You don't want to miss out."

In the time that it took Nick to say his thank-yous and good-nights, someone had wrapped up an entire pie, and Aunt Millie was thrusting it at him. Resigned, he graciously accepted it.

Becca walked with him outside to his car. The temperatures felt as if they'd dipped down below the freezing mark. The weathercasters had warned they would experience the first freezing temperatures of the season tonight. So the chill in the air wasn't solely emanating from Nick.

"That must've been overwhelming for you," she said.

"Just a little bit." He unlocked the car and placed the pie in the backseat.

"It was overwhelming for me, and I've known most of those people all my life."

All he did was smile, but it didn't reach his eyes, and he looked absolutely rung out.

Even so, he hugged her good-night.

While she was in his arms, she breathed in the scent of him, wanting to saturate her senses with it so she could memorize it. Because right now things between them felt fragile and fleeting.

She loved her family in spite of their quirks. Heck, they *were* their quirks. That's what made them unique. They were big and loud and overbearing and brassy, nosy and bossy. God, they could have their own version of the Seven Dwarfs. Although right now, she'd be divested of her role as goody-goody.

She would no longer be thought of as the good girl of the family. It was about time.

Because tonight she'd come to some realizations of her own. Not everyone found her family endearing. And her mother—that bit about making sure she and Nick walked down the aisle before next Thanksgiving—that was inexcusable.

"It's been a long, long day," Nick said. "I need to go. I'll talk to you tomorrow."

"Tomorrow I'm going to be tied up with the tree lighting in the park," she said. "But I hope you'll stop by. It really is pretty. It's a nice way to kick off the holidays."

He didn't say one way or the other if he'd be there tomorrow night, but he did give her a peck on the lips before he got in his car and drove away. And that was something.

Wasn't it?

## Chapter Ten

After Nick left, Becca went back inside her parents' house.

She walked into the kitchen, where her mother was directing the cleanup process.

"Mom, I need to talk to you. Can we please go in the other room?"

"Not now, Rebecca. We need to get this kitchen cleaned up. In fact, there is a whole rack of wineglasses over there that need to be dried and put away. You can sit down while you help. Go do that."

"Mom. The wineglasses will wait. You and I need to have a talk right now. Please, come in the other room, unless you want me to say what I have to say in front of everybody here."

She'd never challenged her mom like this. For the second time that night you could've heard a pin drop, everyone was so taken aback. Even Rosanna. She'd lost her smirk and was watching this showdown unfold with wide eyes.

Isabel glared at Becca for a moment. But then she put down her dish towel, untied her apron and patted her perfect lacquered hair into place.

"If you insist, Rebecca. But make it quick."

The next day, Becca decided to give Nick some space. It wasn't hard, since the foundation tree-lighting ceremony had kept her running all day. Now, as time drew closer for them to flip the switch on the tree and for everybody to *oooh* and *ahhh* and clap their appreciation, everything switched into high gear.

The tree lighting was becoming a nice annual tradition that the entire population of Celebration looked forward to every year. And every year it was getting more and more involved.

The foundation sponsored the event, but this year, they'd added a fund-raising element to benefit the foundation. There was a booth selling Christmas trees, a Christmas shop with ornaments and stockings and other holiday decorations, and a table that encouraged people to think about year-end in giving.

Since this was their first year trying their hand at fund-raising, Becca had been in charge of coordinating the volunteers, in addition to hiring the tree decorator, arranging all the permits and concessions, the carolers and the entertainment.

The prancing reindeer from Miss Jeannie's School of Dance were performing in the gazebo right now. An a cappella group dressed in period costume were singing carols over by the tree. Someone had tracked her down to tell her no one had shown up to man the roasted chestnut booth, so they had to pull somebody from the kettle corn and hot spiced cider stations to fill in until the chestnut roaster arrived.

She had just put out that fire when her neighbor Mrs. Cavett, who she'd appointed as a volunteer for the holiday shop in a moment of weakness, sidled up next to her.

"Lovely event, Becca sweetheart. But you know, honey, next year you really should organize better. It's only proper to provide dinner for the volunteers or at least snacks. I'm starving. It was such a bother to have to take our breaks in rotation. You know, if we had food, we could eat right there while we worked. Happy volunteers make for happy sales."

Becca had a fleeting image of Mrs. Cavett and Mrs. Milton huddled around a platter of shrimp cocktail and ignoring the customers while they gorged.

"I'm sorry you're hungry, Mrs. Cavett. I should have recommended that you eat dinner before you came. I didn't even think about snacks, since the shifts are only two hours long."

Mrs. Cavett *tsked*. Then she took a hold of Becca's upper arm as if for emphasis.

"Sweetheart, the mark of a good hostess is to always feed your guests or, in this case, your volunteers."

"The only problem is this is a fund-raiser. We didn't really have a budget for volunteer snacks. But I do appreciate your input. And, hey, maybe next year we can organize a committee to get food donations or maybe the volunteers could each bring some finger food. May I count on you to coordinate the volunteer treats for us next year?"

"Becca, darling, you don't burden your volunteers by asking them to bring food."

She could see this conversation was going nowhere fast. She'd have better luck arranging a Radio City Music Hall gig for Miss Jeannie's dancing reindeer than trying to get Mrs. Cavett to see things her way. Becca swallowed her indignation.

"Thank you for your input, Mrs. Cavett. I'll pass along your helpful notes to next year's committee."

Of course, she was the sole member of next year's committee.

Becca was thrilled to see Mrs. Milton barreling toward them...looking and sounding like a rampant reindeer who had broken loose from Santa's sleigh, in her brown muumuu and jingle bell necklace, complete with matching earrings.

Even before she arrived, it was clear that Mrs. Milton was coming over to join the criticism choir. Becca knew she'd better disengage now before the two women had her cornered.

"Hi, Mrs. Milton. I'm sorry, but I have to run. I have to get over to the stage to make sure everything is in order for the tree lighting."

As she walked away, Becca wondered who was manning the holiday shop, but she knew if she went back to ask she'd never get away.

Instead, she detoured over to the concession area and bought a bottle of water. It was the first moment she'd had since lunch to stop and take a break, and she was tired. She was scanning the crowd to see if she could spot Nick, when she saw Kate, who seemed to have the same idea as she did, only with hot chocolate.

"Someday we are going to hire someone else to

handle this shindig so we can go Black Friday shopping," said Kate.

"Right. Whose brilliant idea was this to do the tree lighting on the day after Thanksgiving?" Becca smiled. "Oh, yeah, her name is Kate Thayer. She's worse than the Grinch who stole Christmas."

"I hear she's fabulous," Kate said. "A true visionary."

Becca rolled her eyes and laughed.

"I haven't had a chance to talk to you all day," Kate said. "How did Thanksgiving with your parents go?"

Becca rubbed her hands over her eyes and sighed. "Which do you want to hear about first? The part where Aunt Millie tried to force-feed Nick pumpkin pie? The one where my mom announced to everyone that she would make sure Nick and I got married before next Thanksgiving? Or the grand finale where I told off my mother?"

Kate's jaw dropped. "And why didn't you invite me to Thanksgiving? This is like Thanksgiving dinner theater. All we had was a boring dinner with turkey and stuffing. Although, the dessert Liam and I shared was particularly delicious this year, if you know what I mean."

Kate waggled her eyebrows.

"And I'm the one who ends up pregnant with twins."

Kate shrugged, and for a moment Becca thought she glimpsed a hint of sadness in her eyes.

"Are you okay?" Becca asked.

"I'm fine. We have about ten minutes before we have to head over to the stage. I want to hear everything. Especially the part about you telling your mother off. I never thought I'd live to see the day that happened.

I'd ask if you'd been drinking, but I already know the answer to that. What happened?"

Becca squeezed her eyes shut for a moment, trying to erase the memory of the bad scene.

She gave Kate the basic rundown.

"...and after we went upstairs, I told her I didn't appreciate the way she kept insisting that Nick and I were getting married. And my mother kept insisting she'd done nothing wrong. And I told her she needed to stop this constant interference because I'm twenty-five years old and she just needs to stop."

"Get out." Kate's eyes were huge, and she'd had her hand over her mouth the entire time Becca had been telling the story. Kate knew Isabel, and she also understood that Becca's confronting her basically amounted to World War Three.

"Do you know what my mother had the nerve to say?"

Kate shook her head. "I have no idea. I'm terrified of your mother. I can't believe you lived to tell the story."

Becca nodded.

"She said my life *needed* a little more interference from somebody with better sense than I had, since I'd gone and gotten myself pregnant."

Kate winced. "Oh, honey, I'm sorry. That's really out of line."

Becca lifted her chin a notch. "It is. As of right now, we're not speaking. But after the numbness wore off, I realized I've been letting her get away with stunts like that my entire life. I've always thought if I just kept my mouth shut, if I did everything right, she'd love me—"

Becca's voice broke. She cleared her throat.

"But I don't think she knows how to love, Kate. Last night was an epiphany. All these years I've been thinking there was something wrong with me. Well, it's not me, and I'm tired of her making me feel like I'm not good enough to earn her love."

Becca felt her eyes start to well, and she swiped at the tears. The realization had been a weight lifted off her shoulders, but with the burden gone, the heaviness had been replaced by a strange sort of emptiness.

Kate put her hand on Becca's arm and gave it a squeeze.

"Dare I ask, how did Nick handle everything?"

Becca shrugged. "I don't know. He left before my mom and I had it out. I haven't talked to him today. He seemed pretty overwhelmed by everything last night. He just got sort of quiet. I told him I'd be here. Told him that he could meet me for the tree lighting if he wanted to. I haven't heard from him."

"Well, that's because he just walked up."

Becca's breath hitched in her chest.

Kate pointed with her head. "He's right over there with Liam and Jake. I'm pretty sure they're waiting for us to finish what we're doing here so we can join them for the tree lighting."

There he was. Standing there with the entire Sunday night football crew, looking as if he'd always been one of them.

Becca glanced at her phone. He hadn't texted her. But he was here. He probably hadn't texted her for the same reason she didn't text him when he was at work. She had a job to do, and he respected that she didn't have time to be on her phone.

It was actually a courtesy.

After all, he was here tonight. If he hadn't wanted to see her, he could've stayed home or at least avoided her friends... But they had become his friends, too.

Becca checked in with the people from the mayor's office, who were on the podium where the mayor would address the citizens of Celebration before pulling the lever that would officially light the Christmas tree for this season. They were all set. She pointed out the area at the right-hand corner of the stage and told them that's where she'd be if they needed anything.

Then she took a deep breath and went down to join her friends. And Nick.

"There you are," he said. "I was beginning to think you stood me up."

He greeted her with a kiss, and everything seemed fine. She was so relieved she wanted to cry.

"I'm glad you're here."

He put his arm around her, and she snuggled into the warmth of him. She couldn't think of any place else she'd rather be than right here with him.

"And two cups for Becca and Nick?" Pepper asked.

"Hey, Pepper. What's going on?" Becca asked.

"Rob and I would like to buy everyone a cup of hot mulled wine. We need to toast the holidays."

"Oh, that's so nice of you. Nick? Would you like some wine?"

"Sounds great, thanks."

"Okay, one each for Becca and Nick."

Becca held up her hand. "None for me, thanks."

"Come on, Becca," said Pepper. "Don't be a party pooper. We need to have a group toast."

"I'll toast with my water. I'm working."

Pepper squinted at Becca. "Kate's working, but she's having wine. When did you become such a teetotaler? You've never turned down a glass of wine—until lately. What's going on with you? Are you pregnant? You are, aren't you?"

"Pepper..." Becca said, unsure of how to answer. After all, they'd told her family. Their friends would find out soon enough. Why not now?

Becca glanced up at Nick, worried that two nights of pregnancy announcements might send him over the edge. But he gave her his lopsided smile and a barely perceptible shrug.

"And what if she is?" he said to Pepper.

Pepper's jaw dropped. "Are you saying what I think you're saying?"

Becca looked at Nick again, fortified by what she saw in his eyes.

"Yes," Becca said.

Pepper unleashed an earsplitting squeal, and then she threw her arms around Becca's neck. "I knew it! I knew it. I knew it. I knew it. Oh, I am so happy for you two."

"So, you've been baiting me with the wine, haven't you?" Becca asked.

Pepper shot her a sly smile. *"Maaaybe."*

"How in the world did you know?" Becca asked.

Kate was a vault. There was no way she'd betray Becca's confidence. That was one of the few constants in the world she could count on.

Pepper shrugged. "Just intuition, I guess."

Becca didn't believe her, and Pepper must've seen it in her eyes—or maybe it was more of that intuition she was claiming to possess.

"Okay, I'll confess I overheard you and Kate talking about it at the office after you got so sick with the food poisoning. After you recovered, I guess I was a little jealous, because I wanted to celebrate with you, too."

"Pepper, I'm sorry. We had to tell my family before we told anyone else."

"I totally understand," Pepper said. "And I am totally going to throw you the best baby shower this town has ever seen."

Nick was quiet. Of course, nobody could get a word in edgewise when Pepper was excited about something. But Becca was learning that Nick tended to stand back and take things in. He had to process them.

As they stood in the glow of the lighted Christmas tree, Nick standing behind her with his arms around her, holding her close, a calming peace settled over her. Last night, after Nick had left her parents' house, things had been so uncertain between them, she'd feared she might never know this peace again. But she'd trusted her instincts, and she'd given him room to think, to process everything.

He'd come back to her.

Of course, they hadn't talked about her family and everything that had transpired last night. She wasn't going to bring it up tonight. Especially after they said goodbye to their friends and went over to the Christmas tree booth and chose a tree together.

As Nick carried it to her car for her, she caught herself pretending that they were a real family. Because maybe they could be...someday.

Right now, theirs might not be the traditional

situation she wished it would be, but it was one of those situations where she had a choice: the glass could be half empty, or it could be half full.

It was her choice, and she chose half full.

So many good things had happened lately. They had been blessed with not one, but two children. The babies had survived the food poisoning. Nick had come back into her life. She had to trust that everything would be okay.

Maybe if she kept repeating the positive over and over, like a mantra, she could will him to love her enough to make it all true.

## Chapter Eleven

"I can't believe Jake and Anna's wedding is tomorrow," Becca said as she unlocked her front door and flipped on the foyer light.

Nick nodded and bent down to pet Priscilla, who had met them at the door.

Tonight's rehearsal dinner and tomorrow's wedding were the last of what seemed like an endless succession of events that had followed one after the other since Thanksgiving at her parents'. It's not that he wasn't glad to be part of the festivities and the celebrations surrounding his new friends' wedding. He was glad everything would be slowing down pretty soon.

At the risk of sounding like a Scrooge, after telling her parents about the babies on Tuesday, telling her extended family at Thanksgiving dinner, telling their friends about the babies at the tree-lighting ceremony on Friday and going to Jake and Anna's rehearsal din-

NANCY ROBARDS THOMPSON 157

ner tonight, Nick was looking forward to getting back to work, where everything didn't feel so out of control.

Truth be told, he was a little weary, feeling as if he was living someone else's life. Because three months ago, if you had asked him what he'd be doing for the holidays, it wouldn't have been any of the events that had been on his social calendar lately.

He'd volunteered to work tomorrow night, but somehow, despite a good number of the hospital's staff attending the wedding, they'd scheduled him off for the night. Becca was in the wedding, so he would've been just as happy working and giving someone else a chance to go, but Jake and Anna wouldn't hear of it. Nick had begun to feel like a miscreant protesting to the contrary.

He followed Becca into the living room. The dog padded along behind him.

The Christmas tree they'd purchased last night was sitting in a stand in the corner. Becca kicked off her high heels. She looked gorgeous in her black cocktail dress. Nick especially enjoyed the view of her curvy little backside when she bent down and plugged something into the wall.

The tree lit up. Nick blinked in surprise, taking it all in. It didn't have any ornaments, but it shone bright with tiny colorful lights.

"Did you put the tree in the stand?" he asked.

"Not all by myself. Kate helped me. You should've seen the two of us. We were like Laverne and Shirley. I'm surprised we didn't end up putting the trunk through the window. But we eventually got it upright and into the stand."

He frowned. "Should you be lifting things like

that, even with somebody else's help? You should've called me."

"Nick, I'm pregnant, not an invalid. I'm fine. The babies are fine. Thank you for being concerned. And just so you don't feel as if you're missing out, I bought some ornaments we can hang on the tree together."

She held up a red sphere that was decorated with a delicate gold pattern. "I got these for us today. I was hoping you'd want to help me decorate the tree. That's why I went ahead and put the lights on. Because you have to do that first before you can put on any of the other decorations."

"I think you need to slow down a little, Becca. Don't wear yourself out."

"I'm fine. I promise I'm listening to my body."

It had been a long time since he'd bothered with a tree. When he was married to Delilah, they'd spent two Christmases together. She'd badgered him until they'd gotten a tree. He didn't blame her for wanting one. Most people observed that tradition. Hell, most people celebrated traditions.

He glanced at his watch. It was nearly ten o'clock. "I'd love to, but could we wait until next week? There's been so much going on, and we still have the wedding tomorrow."

Disappointment flashed in Becca's eyes, but she recovered quickly, smiling at him. "Of course. We've had a lot going on this week. I'm sure you're exhausted."

Now he was beginning to feel like the Grinch.

"How about if we hang a few tonight and the rest next week? Is that a fair compromise?" he asked.

Her face lit up. "I think it's the perfect compromise."

She planted a whisper-soft kiss on his lips and handed him the ornament.

"Hang it anywhere on the tree you'd like."

She turned on some Christmas music.

*Christmas music? It's not even December yet.*

He contemplated teasing her about it, but she disappeared into the kitchen before he could.

Instead, he turned to find a place on the tree for the ornament.

Out of nowhere, a memory swam from the murky recesses of his subconscious. He remembered how his mother waited patiently until the day after Thanksgiving to play holiday tunes. But only because she and his father had come to that agreement. If his dad had had it his way, there would never have been any Christmas music until the week before the holiday. On the flip side of that coin, his mother would've started torturing them with "Frosty the Snowman" and his ilk as soon as the first chill cooled the air.

In a sense, it was their own compromise. Nick hadn't thought about it in years. It was a happy time, before they'd stopped working together and everything had gone so terribly wrong.

Becca returned a moment later with a bottle of wine and one glass and a mug of something in her other hand.

"You know, it's an honor to get to hang the first ornament," she said as she poured the wine. "So consider yourself honored."

She handed him the glass of wine.

"Mark, Rosanna and I used to fight over who got to hang this Santa ornament that had been in our family for as far back as I can remember. My mom used to keep track of whose year it was to hang it. One year she swore it was Mark's turn, but Rosanna kept insisting that Mark had hung it the year before and it was her turn. She tried to grab it away from Mark and ended up knocking it out of his hand. It smashed into tiny pieces, and that was the end of Santa. Isabel made Rosanna clean up the pieces and then sit on the couch. She didn't get to help decorate the tree that year."

"She didn't punish your brother?"

Becca shook her head. "No, because in her eyes, he hadn't done anything wrong. Rosanna killed Santa. I don't think either of them has forgiven the other."

"So for the most part, you are like the Switzerland of your family. You seem to be a pretty calming influence on everyone."

Becca shrugged. "Somebody has to be. If not, either we'd not be speaking to each other, or we'd be living our life in constant turmoil."

She grimaced.

"What's wrong?"

"Actually, my mother and I are in a bit of a tiff right now."

"What happened?"

Becca took a deep breath, staring off into the distance for a moment. "After you left Thursday, I told her she was out of line for pushing the issue of us getting married. I'm sorry she did that."

Nick waved her off. "Don't worry about it. I think she was just a little overzealous. No hard feelings on my part. So don't let it put you in a bad place with your mother. Go back to being Switzerland."

"We will get past it. I'll just give her a little bit of

space right now. Speaking of parents, when do you want to tell your father about the babies?"

He hadn't even thought about it. Well, he'd thought about it, but he hadn't come to any conclusion. They'd been on the go so much that he hadn't had a chance to think much beyond Thanksgiving dinners and tree lightings and weddings.

"I don't know, Becca."

He hadn't meant for the words to come out quite so sharp. But they had, and Becca was frowning.

"I'm sorry about that," he said. "I haven't seen my father in years. So there's a little more to it than calling him up and telling him he's going to be a grandfather."

Becca nodded.

"What would you think of inviting him to come for Christmas? We could tell him about the babies together and in person."

Nick took a long sip of his wine, weighing his words before he spoke. But all he could come up with was "I don't know."

She put a hand on his arm. "Remember what you said to me. It's all in how you set the tone. And could you think of a better Christmas gift to give somebody than to tell him he's going to be a grandfather?"

The guy hadn't been a particularly great father. Nick wasn't sure how his dad would react to being a grandfather. *The stubborn old coot.*

Becca must have mistaken his shrug for an *I'll think about it.*

"If this is something you want to do, we need to book his airfare soon. It could be our Christmas present to him."

Nick held up a hand. "Whoa, wait there. I don't even know if he would come. I'm guessing he still works." Nick shrugged again. "That's how little I know about him."

Becca was looking at him. She wasn't exactly frowning, but her brows were knit, and those gorgeous full lips were pursed.

"I know you probably think that's crazy," he said. "But that's just the way things are between him and me. I don't like it. But he hasn't seemed too bothered by it all these years, either."

"Don't you think now is as good a time as any to initiate a peace offering It's Christmas, Nick."

After all these years he'd never considered the logistics of being the one to extend the olive branch. Sure, there'd been times when he'd wondered what it would be like to see his old man again after all of these years, but that was usually where it stopped. He couldn't envision himself reaching out to make the first move toward reconciliation. Not when there was a very high chance that his father would reject him all over again.

"Yeah. I don't know about that, Becca. It's really not as easy as simply setting the tone. It's complicated."

"Nick, what could have happened that was so horrible that you can't put it behind you? What did he do to you?"

"It wasn't what he did to me. Well, I mean, if you don't count the way he abandoned my mother and me."

Becca watched him expectantly, as if certain he would continue. But the truth was he didn't know how to explain. He didn't know where to start. He wanted to tell her to not push him. That he and his dad weren't like her and her family. But he knew that would sting. It would hurt her, and it would only make him feel worse.

Still, he heard himself talking before he realized what he was doing.

"When I was fourteen, I went on a cruise with my family. My parents were arguing about something, I don't even know what. But they sent my brother, Caiden, and me down to the pool while they worked things out. My mom told me to look after my brother, but I was distracted, and flirting with a girl. Caiden kept pestering me. 'Hey, Nicky, look at this! Hey, Nicky, watch me! Hey, Nicky, are you gonna kiss that girl?' I got mad at him, and I told him to go away. I just wanted him to go away for a few minutes and leave me alone. Ten minutes later, a swimmer pulled my little brother out of the deep end of the pool. He drowned. I was supposed to take care of him, but I didn't. He drowned because of my carelessness. When my parents found out, for a split second, I saw this look in my mom's eyes. I knew she blamed me even though she never said a word. She blamed me. It was my fault."

Becca reached out and took Nick's hand.

"I'm so sorry, Nick. That must've been horrific."

Her words hung in the air between them, heavy and still.

"But you were only fourteen years old," she said. "Who puts that kind of responsibility on the shoulders of a kid?"

Nick shook his head. "I was old enough to know

better. I did know better. He couldn't swim. But I never thought he'd go near the deep end of the pool."

Nick still had nightmares of them pulling his brother out of the water. Twenty-one years later, and the image was still burned into his brain as if it happened yesterday.

"How long after your brother's accident did your parents divorce?"

Nick leaned forward, bracing his elbows on his knees, studying the grain in the hardwood floors. The song on the stereo changed to "Silent Night."

How long had it been?

"Five, six months, maybe? I think they tried to make it work for me or maybe out of habit or obligation. In so many ways it seemed like they split the moment they found out about Caiden. My dad ended up moving out. I came home from school one day, and he was gone. My mom was a shadow of herself. She just went through the motions. She didn't cry. She didn't talk much. A year later she died. An aneurism. It was as if all her grief had bottled up inside her and exploded. God, I've never told anyone this before."

"Not even your ex-wife?"

"Delilah and I were married for less than two years. She was too busy complaining about how many hours I was away from home to worry about something like this."

They sat there quietly for a while. He felt her gaze on him, but he couldn't look at her. He didn't want to see the pity in her eyes.

Pity had been one of the worst things he'd had to deal with after they returned home, and all the neighbors found out.

Whispers and pity.

*Their family is never going to be the same.*

*Oh, that poor Ciotti boy.*

He was never really sure if they were talking about him or his brother. It had to be Caiden, because he knew he didn't deserve any pity.

"Nick, it wasn't your fault. You have to stop blaming yourself. And most of all, you need to forgive yourself. You were just a kid."

It was all just one more thing that made him feel out of control of his life—babies on the way, a new town that had already sucked him into a way of living he wasn't used to. But he should like it. He should love being part of something bigger than himself. He should welcome a reason to step outside of himself. He knew that.

This was Becca's life. She was at the center of it all. Heart and soul and lifeblood. She thrived in the midst of friends and community and even family, no matter how dysfunctional she thought hers was.

Here he was, trying to be part of it, part of her life. But, really, he was standing on the outside looking in.

It seemed so much bigger than him. It was all coming at him so fast. When it came down to it, could he really give her what she needed to be happy? He wished he could. He wanted to. But she deserved better. Was it fair to her to hold on to her if he couldn't give her all that?

He knew he could sit there all night banging his head against the proverbial wall and telling himself this life should be what he wanted, that he should feel lucky, but he just wanted to run.

He set his wineglass on the coffee table and stood up.

"Look, it's late," he said. "I need to go into the hospital tomorrow and check on some things before the wedding. I need to go."

The next evening, Nick sat in the ballroom at Regency Cypress Plantation and Botanical Gardens waiting for the wedding to start.

Since Becca had been tied up with bridesmaid duties all day and he'd had to take care of a few matters at the hospital, Becca had ridden to the Regency Cypress with Kate. He'd met her there.

In the midst of the rush of all the festivities, Nick hadn't had a chance to get Anna and Jake a wedding present. So, before the wedding he'd swung by the mall to pick up a gift. While he was there, he'd found his way back to the jewelry store where Becca had tried on the ruby necklace. He'd gotten it for her.

He wasn't much of a shopper. So, he figured he might as well pick up the necklace for her Christmas present.

The only other time he'd bought jewelry for a woman was when he'd purchased Delilah's wedding ring. Since they'd eloped, there'd been no engagement ring. Just functional, plain gold his-and-hers bands.

Shortly after the wedding, Delilah had taken to purchasing her own jewelry. That way, she told him, he didn't have to worry about it, and she got exactly what she wanted. She always made sure she got exactly what she wanted.

Sitting here, alone in a sea of people, Nick wondered if the necklace was a good idea. Did buying jewelry for a woman send the wrong message?

It was just a necklace. It wasn't as if he'd bought her a ring.

The string quartet began playing a classical tune that Nick recognized but couldn't name—maybe "Ode to Joy" or that one by Pachelbel, maybe something else. It was pleasant, and for the first time in days—perhaps even since he and Becca had reconnected and he'd learned he was going to be a father—he sat back and took a deep breath.

Liam was one of Jake's groomsmen. He and Jake's three brothers, whom Nick had met briefly at the rehearsal dinner last night, stepped out and took their places beside Jake at the front of the ballroom.

He'd have to remind himself to rib Liam about cleaning up well and about making him miss the football game tonight.

The musical ensemble shifted into another familiar but unidentifiable piece, and a couple of tiny girls in white dresses with deep red sashes tottered down the aisle carrying baskets that were nearly as big as they were and scattering handfuls of flower petals.

One decided to stop midway along the journey to the altar, blinking at the people all around her. She looked as if she was about ready to burst into tears, but the other little girl, who looked as if she might be a year or two older, walked back and took her by the hand and restarted her journey.

The guests *awwed* and *cooed* at the adorableness. Nick stewed in the thought that weddings as a general rule were daunting.

After seeing his parents' marriage go up in flames and failing at his own attempt, he'd probably stop midway to the altar and question what he was doing, too.

Becca was the first bridesmaid to walk down the aisle.

She looked beautiful in the clingy red dress that hugged her in all the right places. She caught his eye as she marched past and smiled. He smiled back. An unexpected warmth started in his solar plexus and radiated outward. What was it about this woman? She had his mind performing a one-eighty every time he saw her. Just a minute ago, he'd been thinking how he wasn't cut out for marriage, that he couldn't be a family man or be part of a close-knit community. Yet every time he set eyes on her, something inside him wanted to recalibrate his life compass and see if it might point to a different true north.

Anna was a beautiful bride as she walked down the aisle on her father's arm. And when Jake swiped at a tear as his father-in-law gave Anna's hand to him, Nick had to admit he couldn't remember seeing anyone look as happy.

The minister called the dearly beloved together and said a few words about guests being fortunate to witness the joining of these two souls.

"I only wish Jake's father and mother could be here today," said the minister. "Jake, your father was a good friend of mine, and I know both of your parents are here in spirit. I know they're thrilled that these two are being joined in holy matrimony, since they knew Anna practically all of her life, too.

"On this Thanksgiving weekend, I urge everyone to hold loved ones close. If there's someone you haven't talked to, call them."

Nick thought of his father. He really did owe it to him to reach out to him and tell him about the babies. Becca's words about forgiving himself rang in his head.

He knew it was true.

He watched the kind, smart, beautiful woman who was carrying his children. He wondered for a moment if there was something wrong with him.

Because surely, if he couldn't love her, he didn't deserve love. She was right, he needed to forgive himself before he could move on and love anyone else.

The first step to forgiveness started with contacting his father.

"I have a surprise for you," Nick said after he put a basket of garlic bread on the table and took his place across from Becca.

"Dinner and a surprise?" she asked.

Nick had already surprised her by calling her this morning and asking if he could cook dinner for her tonight. Apparently, spaghetti and homemade meatballs was his specialty, and he wanted to make it for her.

Here they sat, in his tiny studio apartment, a single white taper candle lit between them, with delicious food on the table and the smell of garlic and Italian seasoning hanging in the air.

"How would you like to meet my father?" Nick asked.

"What? When? I'd love to meet him. Did you call him?"

Nick nodded and smiled.

"And?" she demanded. "Tell me everything."

Nick braced his elbows on the table and laced his fingers together. "The more I thought about it, the more I realized you were right. I owed it to him to tell him about the babies."

She waited a moment for him to continue, but when he didn't, she said, "How did that go?"

A look of tenderness passed over Nick's face. It was an expression she hadn't seen before, and she was a little mesmerized.

"Better than I expected," he said. "It was a little strained at first. I mean, it's been sixteen years since we last talked. I can't believe he still has the same phone number. But he does. He said it was good to hear from me. That he thought about me often and wondered where I was."

Becca had to wonder why the man hadn't tried to get in touch with his son. Surely he didn't blame Nick for what happened to Caiden. But people had their own quirks and ways of dealing with heartbreak.

"I asked him to come. Told him I'd send him a ticket. He wants to meet you. The only thing is, he's flying in the day we are supposed to tour the Dallas hospital."

Becca held up her hands. "That's okay. We can reschedule."

Nick shook his head. "No need. He lands in the evening. We can go to the airport after the tour and pick him up. Would you be up to having dinner with us?"

"Of course, I'd love to. Thank you."

Becca's first thought was *Nick is introducing me to his father.* But then the voice of reason set in. He hadn't seen the man in sixteen years.

"But are you sure you don't want to meet with him first? So the two of you can have some time alone to catch up? I could meet you for dessert or maybe lunch the next day? Is he staying with you?"

Nick glanced around the room. "No. I'm pretty picky about who I share a bed with. I made a reservation for him at the Celebration Inn."

She thought about how he'd been right there with her to break the news about the babies to her parents. Even though Nick had already told his father, she wondered if maybe he wanted her there for a little reinforcement during the first meeting.

She reached out and took his hand. "Nick, I'm so happy for you. It has to be a good sign that he's willing to come and see you."

Nick shrugged. "At least it's a step in the right direction."

On the day of the hospital tour when Becca's phone rang she thought Nick was calling to say that he'd arrived and was waiting outside her office to pick her up for the drive to the hospital.

She picked up her phone with one hand and answered the call as she closed out of the computer file that she'd been working on with the other.

"Becca, it's Nick. I'm sorry to do this at the last minute, but can you meet me at Southwestern Medical Center? I had a hectic morning. We were pretty busy, and then a reporter showed up wanting to interview me for an article about aortic dissection. I should have asked her to reschedule, but I didn't and it ended up going a lot longer than I expected. If I pick you up, we'll be late."

Becca closed the folder on her desk and glanced at her watch. "No problem. I'll meet you there at four.

Unless you want to reschedule, or you know, I could just have the babies at Celebration Memorial. That would be easier on everyone. Lots of healthy twins are born there every day, Nick."

"Unless an emergency happened, and they couldn't give you the treatment that you'd need."

She loved the way he got all protective and puffed up when it came to making sure she got the very best OB care possible, but was this specialty hospital really necessary?

"Nick, think about it," she said. "What would happen if there was an emergency? Couldn't they just put me in an ambulance and send me to Southwestern Medical Center?"

He was quiet on the other end of the line, and for a moment she thought they'd been disconnected.

"Nick?"

"Yep."

She was beginning to see a pattern: when he got stressed, he became very uncommunicative.

"Look," she said, "I understand that you're busy, but taking this tour seems like a lot today with your dad coming in. Let's make him our priority and reschedule."

"My children are my priority——"

"They're mine, too, Nick. I hope you're not questioning that. I'm just trying to keep things in perspective."

"The tour was arranged as a professional courtesy," he said, as if he hadn't heard her. "I'm not going to ask for a reschedule at this late date."

*Fine. Got it.*

His *children* were his priority. He'd made that exceedingly clear. Good grief, this guy could run hot and cold. One minute he was talking about introducing her to his father—and she thought that just maybe he might feel something for her, too. And the next minute there were reality checks like this that shifted everything into perspective and reminded her that she shouldn't let her heart get carried away. Even though it already had.

"Okay," she said. "I'll meet you at Southwestern at four o'clock."

Five minutes later, as Becca was waiting at the elevator to leave the office, Kate appeared with her purse on her arm.

"Fancy meeting you here," Kate said. "Is Nick here to pick you up for the appointment?"

Becca took a deep breath. "No. I'm meeting him there. Some things came up at the hospital, and if he picks me up, we'll be late. Where are you off to?"

"I have an appointment with the superintendent of schools to talk about the foundation funding Get Lost In A Book Week. Are you okay? You seem a little rattled."

Becca shrugged. "Nick's father is arriving tonight. I'm sensing that he might be a little nervous about that, though he won't admit it."

It was either nerves, or Nick was pulling away. Or maybe she was superimposing her own anxiety onto Nick. The only thing she knew for sure was that she would be glad when the hospital tour was over. Maybe then she'd have more clarity about whether or not she was comfortable delivering at Southwestern Medical Center. Nick was a doctor. She knew she should trust him, but not at the expense of going against her own instincts. And for some reason her instincts were telling her she wanted to have the babies closer to home.

"He said it's been a long time since he and his father have communicated, right?"

Becca nodded. Nick had been increasingly hot and cold since Thanksgiving and the string of festivities in between.

"Sometimes he's hard to read, and other times I worry that I am reading too much into our relationship."

Kate's brows knit together. "He acted fine at the tree lighting, and he was attentive at the wedding. From my perspective, you two looked like a couple. A cute couple, as a matter of fact. And now he's introducing you to his father. Of course, I'm not you, but it looks to me like you have yourself a boyfriend."

Becca rolled her eyes at her friend. "A boyfriend. What does that even mean?"

What did it mean? She would certainly like to know.

"I never took you for somebody who needed to slap a label on a relationship," Kate said.

"I'm not looking for a label. But I am looking for answers."

She gazed at her friend. If there was anyone in the world Becca could confide in, it was Kate. The elevator arrived, and the two stepped inside.

As soon as the doors shut, Becca said, "I could really fall for this guy, Kate. I guess I'm just protecting my heart."

Kate's expression turned tender. "Could fall for the guy or *have fallen* for the guy? I'm guessing the latter."

Becca shrugged, not ready to say the words out

loud. Maybe she wasn't even ready to admit it to herself. So she changed the subject.

"Maybe it would be a good idea for me to let him meet with his father alone tonight. I mean, they haven't seen each other in years. Maybe I should give them a little time? What would you do?"

They stepped off the interior elevator and walked together across the lobby toward the lift that would take them to the parking garage.

"Did you ask him if that's what he wanted?" Kate asked.

"I did."

"What did he say?"

"He wants me to come with him."

"Well, there you go. Let him make that call. Unless you're the one who is having doubts."

"Me? Not a chance. I was the one who urged him to call his dad and tell him about the babies. I wanted to pay for part of his ticket as a Christmas present from the two of us, but when I asked him about it, he skirted the issue."

Kate grimaced. "Do you want me to be honest?"

"Always."

"Don't make an issue where there's not one."

"I'm not making an issue of it. I just thought he might wait so we could tell him together. I thought we were bringing him here to tell him about the babies, but Nick told him on the phone when he talked to him…"

"Are you disappointed that he told him without you?"

"No. Well, sort of, I guess…but that's selfish. I know that, and I wouldn't admit it to anybody but you. I guess I thought it would be similar to when we told my parents together."

The truth was, he had gone with her as moral support—not because they were the happy, loving couple giddy about sharing joyous news. Things were different with his dad. Realistically, Nick probably needed an opener, a reason for calling his dad. When you haven't spoken with somebody in nearly two decades, *hello, how have you been?* doesn't always get it. *You're going to be a grandfather* does a lot better cutting through the minutia.

"I'm a big girl. I understand why he did what he did. Now I guess this trip is more about the two of them, and that's great."

"But his dad wants to meet you. Or Nick wants to introduce you."

"Right. He does. Or so Nick said. But since he's already told him we're expecting, this trip is more about them healing their relationship and making things right between them. I'm all for that. It has to happen before anything else can be right. He's only here for two nights. I just don't want to cut into their time."

Kate smiled at her. "You're going with him. Be glad about it, and everything will be fine."

Kate hugged Becca.

"I don't mean to give you a hard time. I just wish you'd stop giving yourself such a hard time."

In the car, Becca grappled with her feelings. Kate was right. She was always so logical. Becca needed to stop reading more into this than was really there. She needed to ignore the hollow feeling that wanted to consume her. In fact, when she felt too empty and off-kilter, she knew that's when she needed to erase her mental Etch A Sketch and focus on the positive.

As she drove to meet Nick, though, she should've been focusing on the car to her right. If she had been, maybe she would've been able to stop before it ran the stop sign and hit her car.

## Chapter Twelve

By the time Nick got the news that Becca had been in an accident, he was already at Southwestern Medical Center in Dallas, waiting for her, wondering why she was late when she was usually early.

Kate had called him and told him she'd been in a fender bender. She'd witnessed the accident. Apparently, a teenager had been texting and ran a stop sign and hit the right fender of Becca's Honda. The boy hadn't been going very fast, but as a precaution, Becca had been transported by ambulance to Southwestern Medical Center, where she'd been examined.

Even though Kate had assured Nick that the accident wasn't serious, as he waited, Nick was in a numb haze.

Thank God for air bags and seat belts.

Several hours later, after the doctor had released

Becca and assured him that she and the babies were fine, he'd insisted on driving her home. Kate had put her car back in the parking garage. He told Becca he'd drive her to work tomorrow and they'd make arrangements to take her car into the body shop to be fixed. But on the way home from the hospital, realization set in. If he'd picked up Becca as he'd promised, rather than being so consumed with talking to that damn reporter, this would've never happened. He could've gotten her and his children killed by not following through. She hadn't even wanted to go on the blasted tour. This would've never happened if he hadn't been so focused on himself and so insistent on not inconveniencing his colleague at Southwestern Medical Center.

He felt Becca's gaze on him, but he kept his eyes glued to the road, not wanting to have a wreck be the cause of Becca being in two accidents in one day.

Wouldn't that just be par for his course?

In his life, tragedy seemed to appear in pairs. His brother had died and his parents divorced. Delilah had divorced him and married his best friend. Because he didn't pick Becca up, she'd gotten into that accident. He'd be damned if he was going to look away even for a second and endanger her again. He drove with extraordinary care to keep the pattern from repeating itself today.

He didn't expect life to be strife-free. Ups and downs were a part of the package. The down times made the good times better.

But the rough times in his life—the times that had produced the worst despair, Caiden's death, his parents' divorce, Delilah sleeping with his friend—

it all could've been prevented if he'd just done the right thing.

Now the right thing seemed that Becca and the babies would be better off without him. He'd provide support, of course, but he really was starting to believe he would be of more service to them if he focused on his job and didn't try to have much of a personal life.

He'd said it before, he was married to his work, and medicine was a jealous spouse. The ER seemed to be the place where he did the most good and wreaked the least amount of havoc.

"I keep waiting for you to tease me about the lengths I'd go to to get out of that hospital tour," Becca said.

He nodded, and he thought he smiled—he meant to—but he kept his eyes pinned to the road. The town had put up the decorations the day after the tree-lighting ceremony. Now all of downtown Celebration was decked out in its yuletide finest.

"Did your dad's plane get in?"

"It did."

He'd texted him that there'd been an emergency, apologized and told him he'd meet him later at the inn. He purposely left the details vague because he didn't want to worry him. His dad had sounded genuinely delighted when he told him he was going to be a grandfather. Another part of him didn't want to start off this potential reconciliation with the thoughts *so you ruined this relationship, too* wedged in between them like the proverbial elephant in the room.

"Nick?"

*"Hmm?"*

"Did he take a cab to the inn?"

"Yes. I would assume so."

Nick glanced at the clock on the dashboard. It was close to eight o'clock. It was getting a little late for dinner, but he'd get over to the Celebration Inn as soon as he could. As soon as he got Becca settled at home.

"Are you still going to go see him?"

"Yes."

Becca was quiet for a few beats.

"Would you like to see him alone tonight? I'm eager to meet him, but I haven't been able to shake the feeling that maybe it would be best if the two of you met by yourselves first."

"Sure."

"Nick, talk to me." Becca reached out and put her hand on his arm.

"About what?"

"We could start with why you're being so quiet. You've barely said a word since you got to the hospital. The words you have uttered have been all but monosyllabic. Are you mad at me? Because you know the accident wasn't my fault. It was an accident."

He pulled up to a red light, rolled to a slow, gentle stop before looking over at her.

"Of course it's not your fault. That kid ran a stop sign."

The light turned green, and he trained his attention on the road again.

They rode in silence until they got to Becca's condominium complex. Nick parked, got out and walked around to Becca's door, intending to open it, but she'd already let herself out of the car and had started walking toward the door.

*Oh, boy.*

"Becca, wait."

He caught up with her at the door. She was fishing her keys out of her purse.

He suddenly didn't know what to say. He could tell she was upset. Hell, he was upset—not with her, but it had just been one of those days.

With the accident and the fear of losing his children compounded with seeing his father again, which was dredging up all kinds of unwelcome memories, he was starting to feel a little claustrophobic.

And the burning question kept raging through his head: What if she had died? What if they hadn't gotten so lucky and she had died? Like his brother and his mom—

He shook away the thoughts. He couldn't let himself go down that slippery slope. Because once he started, he might not be able to pull himself out.

The attending on duty in the Southwestern ER who had examined Becca had given her the green light. She'd said she felt fine—no bumps and bruises. She'd only been a little shaken, as most people were when they were involved in a minor accident.

Nick knew the best thing he could do for both of them was to give her a chance to rest and him a chance to gather his wits—and he still had to go see his father. Since he was in town for only two nights, Nick couldn't very well bring him here and then blow him off.

Becca had gotten the door unlocked. The porch

light wasn't on and she'd had to use her phone as a flashlight.

He could've helped her instead of standing there with his hands in his pockets, but she was so capable, so strong—so better off without him.

He took a step back. She took a step inside. Priscilla ran around in circles as she barked a greeting. When Becca turned to look at him, hurt, anger, confusion—probably all of that and more—clouded those beautiful blue eyes.

He should hug her.

He wanted to hug her.

Why couldn't he move toward her? What the hell was wrong with him? He had no idea, which proved that it would be best for both of them for him to clear his head before he did something irreparably stupid.

"Get some sleep," he said.

She shook her head and closed the door, leaving him standing there in the dark.

The last time Nick had seen his dad, the two of them had exchanged words. In his junior year of high school after his mom had died, and Nick had gone to live with his father, Nick had admittedly been a little hard to handle.

Ronnie Ciotti had been a tough customer. Blue-collar from his crew cut to his work boots, Ronnie had been an electrical worker, a union man, a wiry guy with a fierce temper who played by the rules and expected no less from his smart-ass son.

After Nick's parents had divorced, Ronnie hadn't come around much. Back in the day, Nick had taken it personally, on behalf of himself and his mom. But now with the clarity that hindsight offered and the perspective that came from maturity, he realized the divorce must have been just as hard on his father as it had been on his mother.

Ronnie Ciotti didn't like to lose. From this vantage point, it must've been damn difficult to lose his entire family the way he had.

This afternoon, Nick had glimpsed a similar feeling when for several excruciating moments he hadn't known Becca's condition after Kate had called him to tell him about the accident. She wouldn't have told him the worst of it over the phone.

The sad thing was, he'd prepared himself for the bottom to fall out of everything. He'd braced himself for that sickeningly familiar feeling of having someone he loved ripped away from him, having his heart torn right out of his chest and thrown on the floor. When it didn't happen, when he'd realized Becca and the babies were fine—and he was so grateful they were—he also realized he didn't want to render himself so vulnerable.

He'd make a terrible father, anyway. If he kept his distance, he could provide for them without actively screwing up their lives.

Over the years, he'd managed to keep from getting involved. Now he knew why. When you opened yourself to love—especially with someone like Becca—you opened yourself to potential pain and loss. That realization made him want to retreat back into his world of emergency medicine, where he was good at what he did, where he could fix people but not have to get involved. In the emergency room he had control over most things—not all things, but he was removed from the things that were out of his control, the losses faced by other people at the cruel hands of fate.

Nick walked into the lobby of the inn and looked around for his father. He'd texted him as he was leaving Becca's, saying he'd be there within ten minutes. It was after eight-thirty now. If the guy hadn't gotten himself something to eat, he must be starving by now.

"Welcome to the Celebration Inn," said a perky redhead who was manning the desk. "Are you staying with us tonight?"

"I'm meeting someone."

Nick had no idea what he was walking into, if his dad still had the same volatile temperament, or if he'd mellowed over the years. It was just nerves on Nick's part, he knew it. The knot in his stomach was testament to that. Besides, would the guy have come all the way from Florida to Texas just to have words with him? He could've done that over the phone; he could've hung up on him. Nick reminded himself his dad had been agreeable.

Maybe time had mellowed him.

The front desk clerk motioned toward an adjacent doorway. "You might want to check the sitting area."

When Nick entered the room, he caught a glimpse of someone sitting in a chair in the corner reading a newspaper and sipping a cup of something that Nick assumed was coffee. The room smelled as if someone had just brewed a pot.

"Dad?"

The guy looked up and smiled, and it reached all the way to his dark eyes. He looked a little older, and he'd gone a little soft around the middle. There was more gray than brown in his close-cropped curly hair, but Nick could see back through the years to the man he hadn't talked to in nearly two decades.

Ronnie stood and offered his hand. Nick shook it.

"Son, it's good to see you."

"You, too. Thanks for coming all this way. Are you hungry?"

Ronnie nodded. "I could eat a bite. But where is your lady? Isn't she coming with us?"

Nick glanced around the quaint sitting room, at the white wicker furniture that looked more decorative than comfortable despite the bright floral-patterned pillows that covered the seats and backs.

He was suddenly exhausted and couldn't bear the thought of having to explain the accident. Becca and the babies were fine. He and his dad had so many other things to discuss.

"She couldn't make it tonight," he said. "Maybe tomorrow, though. We'll see. We'd better get going. Celebration rolls up the sidewalks at ten o'clock. Are you up for walking? The place I have in mind is just down the street."

"I've been sitting so much today, a walk would do me some good."

The inn was located right across from Central Park. As they walked out the front doors toward the restaurant, the lit Christmas tree caught Nick's eye. His thoughts tumbled back to the night of the tree-lighting ceremony and how right Becca had felt in his arms and how happy their friends had been learning the news.

Everyone seemed to be taking the news well, actually—not that it should matter if anyone didn't. It wasn't anybody's business but his and Becca's. Why was it, though, that Nick still couldn't seem to wrap his mind around parenthood and fatherhood? What was wrong with him? But the even bigger question was, how come every time he allowed himself to get close to someone, tragedy struck?

He was a scientist. He wasn't superstitious. But sometimes you just had to look at the writing on the wall.

The accident was his fault. He shouldn't have insisted that they go to Southwestern. The fact that Becca and the babies had escaped unscathed was making him think that maybe they'd be better off if he took a more hands-off approach.

Maybe he just needed some space to think and to figure things out. But first, he needed to catch up with his dad.

"That's a nice Christmas tree over there in the park," Ronnie said. His deep voice was a little gravellier than it used to be. He hoped his dad had kicked the cigarette habit. He hadn't smelled like smoke, the way he used to—Ronnie's aftershave had always mixed with the smell of cigarette smoke, creating a close, almost suffocating calling card that had permeated their whole apartment.

"Yeah, this is a nice, close-knit little town. The residents take a lot of pride in doing things like that. In fact, the foundation that Becca works for was instrumental in organizing the tree lighting. The whole town turned out for it."

Ronnie nodded. "That Becca of yours sounds like quite a woman. I hope I get to meet her while I'm here. I don't know when I'll make it back for a visit.

Then again, maybe the two of you could come and visit me in Florida."

Nick's first thought was *maybe after the babies were born*, but he didn't know what their situation would be. But things seemed to be going well with his father, and Nick was hesitant to introduce any bit of negativity.

Instead of answering, Nick gave a noncommittal nod. By that time, they'd reached Taco's, Nick's favorite restaurant in downtown Celebration.

Nick approached the hostess stand. "Are you still seating for dinner?"

The blond smiled at him as she gathered up two menus. "Yes sir, we are happy to seat people until 10:00 p.m. I have a table available for you. Please, follow me."

The place wasn't very busy, so they'd no more than settled in when the server came over and took their drink orders—cold draft beer for both of them. Then they were both quiet as they perused the menu.

Taco's was located near the square, and it was his default restaurant when his refrigerator was bare or he was short on time and needed to pick up something quickly—which was most of the time.

He ordered the chicken enchilada platter. His dad, the same. It struck Nick as a little odd that Ronnie, who had always been so full of strong opinions and my-way-or-the-highway stances, seemed to be deferring to his son. It was only beer and enchiladas, but Nick couldn't remember a time when the guy he'd always butted heads with deferred to anyone.

With their orders placed and the cold mugs of beer

in hand, the two of them began the slow, cautious journey of catching up.

Of course, they'd both been busy. Ronnie was still working, even though he'd moved from San Antonio to Florida. He'd wanted a change of scenery—a new start.

"It's really good to see you, son. You've done a good job. Really made something of yourself. You're my idea of a self-made man."

Nick didn't know about that. He made a good salary and he saved a good portion of it, but he certainly wasn't Rockefeller rich. That was his idea of a self-made man. But he could see why he might think that. He took a lot of pride in not asking anyone for help. He liked his job. Did he like his life?

Until he'd met Becca and moved to Celebration, he hadn't really had a life outside of work. Maybe that's one of the things that was plaguing him, making him question what should be the best thing that had ever happened to him.

The truth was Nick thrived on change in work environments, but personally, in much the same way that he always returned to the chicken enchilada platter at Taco's, he found comfort in the sameness of his personal life.

Becca stirred things up. Not in a malicious way, more like holding up a mirror so that he could see his life reflected back at him. It had thrown him out of his comfort zone and into chaos.

But the truth was, if not for her, he probably wouldn't be sitting here with his father right now. They were both stubborn men. Who knew if either of them would've ever made the first move toward reconciliation if not for Becca.

*You have to forgive yourself before you can move on.*

The comfort of sameness was an illusion. It was also a bandit that robbed you of time and relationships you might never recover.

*You have to forgive yourself...*

"What happened, Nicky?" Ronnie asked.

The question threw Nick, because the last time he could remember his father calling him Nicky was before Caiden died.

"Why have we not spoken in all these years?"

A silent growl of defensiveness wanted to pop off something smart-assed and hard-edged. But he wasn't seventeen years old anymore.

Ronnie must've mistaken his silence for blame, because he said, "Whatever it is that I did to you—it's been so damn long ago that I don't even remember—I'm sorry."

Nick hardly recognized the man sitting across the table from him. His father was apologizing?

Apologizing. And it sounded as if he was willing to shoulder the brunt of the blame. That wasn't right.

"It was my fault. I should never have taken my eyes off Caiden. If I'd done what I was supposed to do, he'd still be alive and I'm sure our lives would've all turned out differently. Mom might still be here—or at least I'd like to think she would, because the two of you probably wouldn't have gotten a divorce—"

Ronnie held up his hand. "I loved your mother. I don't want you to ever think that I didn't. But our marriage had been in trouble for a long time. We just worked hard to hide it from you and Caiden. The cruise was supposed to get our relationship back on track. But it didn't."

"Well, it might have if Caiden hadn't died. And that's my fault."

Ronnie stared at Nick for several beats. "Son, I know you blamed yourself after everything happened. I even lied to myself and thought that the reason you needed to get away was because losing your brother was just too painful. It was hard on all of us. But one thing I know right now, sitting here with you, is that I made a mistake letting you go away with so much guilt in your heart. If anyone was to blame, it was your mother and me for allowing you to shoulder the responsibility of your brother. You were just a kid. And you need to know your mother and I never blamed you."

Nick's instinct was to throw up the shutters. To clam up and retreat deep inside where he didn't have to deal with these feelings. He'd spent a good portion of his life burying them because they were simply too painful to deal with.

"Of course you blamed me. It was my fault. I was the one to blame, and I will carry that with me for the rest of my life."

Ronnie slapped his hand down on the table. "Well, you're not the only one who has been carrying this guilt with you. How do you think it feels to know if I hadn't been fighting with my wife that day my younger son wouldn't be dead and I wouldn't have ruined your life and driven you away from me? If I hadn't been fighting with your mother, all of our lives might've turned out different."

Strangely, there was an odd comfort…well, maybe not comfort, but it was reassuring to see that his fiery father hadn't completely changed. No, it wasn't comfort. It was a completely new perspective on guilt to which Nick had always thought he owned the exclusive rights.

It was an eye-opener.

He had no idea his dad had been shouldering the burden of blame, too. For the first time since he could remember, he and his father saw eye to eye on something.

But what was he supposed to do with that? It certainly wasn't something he wanted to share a fist bump of solidarity over. They both felt guilty. They both blamed themselves. Arguing over who was guiltier or the bigger schmuck or the worst human being alive wouldn't change anything. It wouldn't bring back Caiden or Mom. It certainly wouldn't give them back the lost years. Nick didn't know what to say.

"You know, your mom and I didn't just lose one son that day." His dad's voice was softer now. "We lost you, too. You were gone long before you left home. And it's taken me all these years to realize that. But after you called me and told me I was going to be a grandfather, it was as if you'd given me back my life. That day last week when I heard your voice, it was as if you'd offered me a new start."

Ronnie paused. Nick wondered if he was waiting for Nick to object or to throw something back at him. But words jumbled and knotted in the back of Nick's throat. He couldn't have said anything, even if he'd known what to say.

"I had to take sick days to come here and see you, but when I heard your voice, I knew I would rather get fired—hell, I would rather die—than waste the chance to make things right with my boy. You and your kids and Becca, if she'll allow me, are the only family I have. Son, I screwed up with your mom. I didn't man up because I was too busy wallowing in my own sadness to let her lean on me. She was the love of my life, and I just let her walk out the door. I let you walk out the door. I was such a self-centered jackass. If I could change one thing in my life, I would go back and make sure your mother knew how much I loved her. And I'd make sure you know how much I regret losing the past sixteen years with you. I hope you know how sorry I am."

Ronnie's voice broke. A tear trailed down his cheek. It cut Nick to the bone because he couldn't remember a single time in his life when he'd seen his father cry.

Not at Caiden's funeral.

Not at his wife's funeral.

Certainly not the day Nick had left home to join the marines.

Or maybe it was the simple act of his father apologizing that was melting the ice that had formed in Nick's heart all these years.

He slid a napkin across the table toward his father. It must've embarrassed him, because the older man said, "Yeah, hey, sorry about this. I'll be right back."

As Ronnie stood up and started to walk away, Nick said, "Dad, I'll make a deal with you. If you forgive me, I'll forgive you. And then we both have to forgive ourselves."

Ronnie stared at Nick for what seemed an eternity. Then he offered a solemn nod before he turned and walked toward the restrooms in the back of the restaurant.

## Chapter Thirteen

Someone was knocking at the door. In fact, Priscilla, the corgi, was going crazy barking and turning in circles as she tried her best to herd Becca off the sofa and into the foyer. It was ten o'clock at night and whoever it was wasn't just knocking, he or she was being rather insistent.

If Priscilla didn't wake the neighbors, her uninvited guest would. Becca rolled her eyes as she thought about the upbraiding she was sure to get from Mrs. Milton and Mrs. Cavett.

But soon enough annoyance gave way to an anxious hopefulness that left her a little queasy as her stomach twisted and plummeted. Maybe Nick had come back to apologize.

As quick as the glimmer of hope appeared, Becca squashed it. She was tired of these ups and downs.

Tired of feeling as if she was walking on eggshells around him. Tired of trying so hard to do everything right. *Dammit.*

"Priscilla, please, be quiet. You're a good watchdog, but I can take it from here."

As if she understood perfectly, Priscilla dropped into a submissive stance—front paws down, corgi butt in the air—and uttered a quieter sound that was more embarrassed yodel than fierce watchdog bark.

"Good girl." Becca bent to give the little dog an appreciative stroke. She was in no hurry to get to the door. If it was Nick, he could stew for a minute. If he didn't want to be with her and his children, they would be better off on their own.

She glanced at the Christmas tree, which was adorned with only the lights Becca had installed and the two ornaments they'd hung—one each. She couldn't even get him to commit to decorating the tree—probably too domestic for him. Not enough emergency room blood and guts. Much too boring and long-term, seeing how she liked to leave up the tree until Epiphany.

She wasn't going to force him to do anything he didn't want to do. If he couldn't come to this relationship table willingly, she sure as shoot fire was not going to beg him.

After the Thanksgiving incident with her mother, whom she still hadn't heard from, and after Nick had gone all stoic and standoffish, Becca had realized she was done earning people's love.

*Done.*

*Finito.*

It was a matter of self-preservation.

She took a moment to gather her thoughts as she slowly made her way to the door. She flipped on the porch light—only so she could get a clear look out the peephole.

One could never be too cautious.

Ha! She should've thought of that before she let herself fall for a guy who had no desire to settle down with a wife and children. With a guy who withdrew to inner Siberia every time life got a little messy.

*Well, you know what, Nick? Life is messy. It can be messy and ugly and unpredictable. People had accidents, and when they survived you were supposed to love them and count your blessings. You weren't supposed to retreat and push them away.*

But if he wanted to back away, that was fine. She wasn't going to chase him and try to convince him that he needed her, that she was worth loving. All her life she'd been the good girl, and all it had gotten her was the expectation that her sole purpose in this life was to please other people.

She was prepared to say those words to him. In fact, she hoped he'd come by so she could tell him everything she'd been thinking since he'd so unceremoniously dropped her off at home after the accident.

However, when she looked out the peephole, it wasn't Nick. It was her mother and Rosanna.

The disappointment that it wasn't Nick was nearly crushing. Becca hated herself for it. She breathed through the sting and hit the mental *save* button on the memo to Nick in her brain.

That's what it was. It wasn't that she wanted to see him so much as she'd wanted the chance to tell him exactly what was on her mind.

Her mother knocked again, or at least Becca assumed it was her mother, because she'd been the one closer to the door. Rosanna had been standing a safe distance behind her.

"Rebecca, are you in there?" her mother called. "Please, open the door."

*Please?*

Had Isabel Flannigan actually ended a sentence with the word *please*?

That was a good sign. Or at least Becca hoped it was a good sign. She'd been through so much today with the accident and Nick going emotionally AWOL, she simply didn't have the energy to go to battle with her mother.

Isabel started pounding again, and Becca jerked open the door, bracing herself for her mother to unleash a tirade about how it was cold outside and Becca had left her standing there. Instead, Isabel threw her arms around her daughter and started sobbing.

*"Mom."*

"Rebecca, I heard you were in an accident. Why on earth didn't you call me?"

This was weird for three reasons—probably even more, but right now Becca was too taken aback to count—1) she and her mother hadn't spoken since Thanksgiving; 2) Isabel *never* made the first move toward reconciliation; and 3) her mother considered any physical displays of affection vulgar.

Yet here she was, practically squeezing the stuffing out of her.

"Are you okay, Rebecca? Colleen Carlton's daughter works at Southwestern Medical Center, and Colleen called me to ask if you were okay. Of course,

I had no idea that you'd even been in an accident. I didn't know what to say. She had to fill me in based on what her daughter had told her."

*Oh. Okay. Here we go.*

Still caught in her mother's embrace, Becca exchanged a look with her sister. To her surprise, it was more concern than the usual disdain.

"But that doesn't matter. You're here, and you're okay." Isabel pulled back, still holding Becca at arm's length, and assessed her daughter.

The sight of her mother standing there with tears streaming down her face, holding on to her as if she were afraid she'd float out into the ether if she let go, liquefied the hard stance Becca had been prepared to take with her mother.

"Mom, I'm fine. Please, don't cry."

"Good luck getting her to listen," Rosanna said. "I was telling her that the whole way over."

Again, Becca braced for Hurricane Isabel to unleash her fury, but this time on Rosanna. Again, she refrained.

"Accidents happen so fast." Isabel's voice was barely a whisper. "If I'd lost you today without being able to talk to you and mend this rift, and I'd never gotten the chance to tell you I'm sorry and I love you, I don't think I could've gone on."

"Mom, I told you. I'm fine. Really, I am. Everything is fine. I'm not mad at you. Please, don't be upset."

So much for the new hard-hearted Becca.

She could stand up for herself, but she didn't have to be mean and heartless. Her mother was so upset, and Becca couldn't bear to see her that way.

"Come in, please," Becca said. "Rosanna, will you please shut the door?"

Her sister, who was also curiously subdued tonight, nodded and did as Becca had asked.

She walked arm in arm with their mother into the living room.

The three of them sat for a moment, looking at each other.

"I'm sorry I didn't call you," Becca said. "I was fine, and I didn't want to worry you."

Isabel drew in a deep breath. "No, I suspect you didn't call me because you were mad at me. And I don't blame you."

She paused and swallowed so hard, Becca could hear her mother's throat working.

"You were right, Rebecca. What I did at Thanksgiving dinner was out of line. I not only embarrassed you and Nick, I embarrassed myself. I hope you will be able to forgive me."

Nick's *ignosces* tattoo flashed in Becca's mind.
*Forgive me.*

The memory of how his hard bicep felt under her fingers, as she'd traced the letters, made her shudder. She blinked away the thought.

"Are you okay?" Isabel asked.

"I am. I'm touched by what you said. As far as I'm concerned, we can put it behind us as long as you realize, Mom, we may not always see eye to eye, but as long as we respect each other, we will be fine. And what I mean by respect is you can't browbeat me into doing things your way."

Isabel straightened in her chair. Her chin lifted a couple of notches in a guarded stance that had Becca bracing for her to go on the defensive. Becca was so tired of fighting. So tired of trying to please everyone that she almost did a double take when her mother said, "I'll behave myself. I promise. And I'd like to apologize to Nick. When can the two of you come for dinner?"

Becca took care not to let her face give away what she was really feeling. Because she didn't know if there would be another family dinner with Nick, but she didn't have to explain that to anyone. At least not right now.

When Nick had learned that his father would be visiting, he'd arranged to take off the whole time he was in Celebration.

When he'd told Cullen Dunlevy why he wanted the time off, Cullen had been generous, telling him to take all the time he needed. Actually, he needed only two nights because he'd been late getting to him last night due to the circumstances of the day.

The morning after their dinner, Nick met his father for breakfast. Afterward, they'd met Cece Harrison, the guide who was giving them a tour of Celebration, sharing some of the lesser known history of the area. The woman who tended the front desk at the Celebration Inn had arranged the tour for them. She'd promised that Cece, who was also a staff writer for the *Dallas Journal of Business and Development*, was not only a friend, but also a knowledgeable local historian. She highly recommended her.

Cece didn't disappoint. She was perky and pretty and everything a person looking to learn more about the town might hope for.

She even tried to flirt a little with Nick, which caused Ronnie to elbow him good-naturedly. But that only made Nick's mind drift back to Becca. Ronnie said, "Don't waste your efforts on him. He's in love."

And he was.

Just like that, Nick knew it. But he had no idea what to do about it.

Cece smiled and cooed about how romantic it was to see someone so much in love and how she wished that someday she'd find someone who was just as smitten with her.

Ronnie joked about applying for the job. It was all good-natured and harmless, since he was old enough to be her father.

"Where's this lucky lady today?" Cece asked.

Both she and Ronnie turned expectant eyes on Nick.

"She's at work." He hoped. He really should've called her to make sure she was okay. But the tour was moving on.

They learned that Celebration was founded in the mid-nineteenth century and had been settled by the Rice family. They stopped in front of the sprawling Victorian mansion that overlooked the east side of the park.

"This was the home of the Rice family," Cece said. "They decided to name the town Celebration because, after months and months of searching, the family had finally found a place to call home, and, of course, this was a great cause for *celebration*."

As Cece and Ronnie joked about her play on words, Nick was struck by how the whole town seemed to be all about family.

The thought of a man sacrificing everything to give his family a safe place to call home made Nick ache with a vast emptiness. What was wrong with him that he couldn't man up for Becca?

He had to admit that his panic over her accident really was just an excuse. It was selfish justification: if he didn't get attached, then he wouldn't hurt those he loved, and in turn he couldn't get hurt himself.

Was he really that weak?

Weren't things with his father so much better than he ever could have hoped for? It was a fresh start for both of them, and it never would've happened if he hadn't taken a chance.

Ronnie was laughing at something that Cece had said, but Nick had missed it, and he didn't want to ask her to repeat herself. His mind was wandering too much to concentrate on the tour.

"There's something I need to take care of," Nick said. "Would you excuse me?"

"Everything okay?" Ronnie asked.

"I hope so," he said. "I'll let you know when I see you tonight at dinner."

Becca should've told Nick no instead of betraying the new stronger, tougher, I'm-tired-of-beating-myself-up-to-win-your-love woman she'd become.

But here she was parking her car in front of Bentleys across the street from the hospital.

Of course she would go to him. Her office was in Dallas and his was right here.

*God*, would she never learn?

Of course, if she'd told him no the first time instead

of spending the night with him, they wouldn't be meeting to have this conversation.

Of course, he'd been cryptic about why he wanted to meet her today. Since he hadn't indicated otherwise, she was going to assume that this meeting was goodbye.

Well, goodbye to any notion of them being a couple or a traditional family. The thought made her heart hurt, but they might as well establish things now. Because the longer they dragged them out, the harder it would be to separate herself.

She'd already let herself fall in love with him, and look where that had gotten her.

As she got out of the car, she squared her shoulders. This would be the last time she would accommodate him. And she intended to tell him that when she saw him.

Her heart felt hollow and fragile. Her eyes burned with the threat of tears that she would not let fall. She couldn't, because if she started crying now, she might not stop.

She couldn't let him see her that way. She knew him well enough to believe he wasn't a cruel man who would take pleasure in watching her suffer.

No, this was more a case of not humiliating herself in front of a man who didn't want her. It was as plain and simple as that. The man she'd fallen in love with didn't love her back. He didn't want her.

That reminder dried up any threat of falling tears. It would be her mantra when she was feeling weak. Her pillar if she felt as if she was starting to fall.

As she pulled open the door to the restaurant, she had another sinking spell. Her mind skipped back to *that night*. That fateful night when she'd accommodated Rosanna's demand for space, and she'd come over to Bentleys to get out of the way.

She'd fallen for him the minute she'd laid eyes on him, and all common sense had gone out the window.

Why had she agreed to meet him here?

As she approached the hostess stand, she reminded herself that it was too late now. She was here—*ohhh*…and there he was sitting at the same booth they'd shared that night.

She took back the benefit of the doubt that she'd afforded him. Because choosing that table just seemed cruel.

When he'd called and asked if she could meet him there, she'd assumed that he was asking for his convenience. So he could get back to the hospital fast.

Now she wasn't sure.

In fact, she wasn't sure of anything except that she should've insisted on him meeting her halfway between Dallas and Celebration. In the future, when they had to see each other for a matter that had to do with their children, she would make sure that they split the difference the same way they would split everything else—expenses, holidays with the kids…

"I see the person I'm meeting," Becca said to the hostess, taking care to smile and temper her voice so as not to misdirect her frustrations.

When Nick saw her, he stood, offering a half smile.

Damn him for being so good-looking and so cool about the situation. Especially when she was falling apart inside. She swallowed the lump in her throat, determined to not let him see just how hard this was for her.

When she reached the booth, there was an awkward moment where neither of them seemed to know what to do. For a split second, she actually thought he might lean in and kiss her. But that was just wishful thinking.

She ducked her head and slid into the booth. He did the same.

"How are you?" he asked.

"I'm fine, Nick. How are you? How's your dad?"

Yes, that was the key. Keep it light. Make him believe she really was fine. Maybe if she pretended long enough, she really would be.

"My dad is— He's great. We've had some good talks. Can't thank you enough for pushing me to get in touch with him."

*Pushing him?*

Is that how she'd come across? Pushy? She cringed inwardly, but she was careful to not let it show. Or at least she hoped she didn't. She certainly hadn't realized she'd pushed him.

"Nick, I'm sorry if you ever felt like I pushed you. I was never trying to force you into anything. That was never my intention."

"I guess that didn't really come out the way I meant it to. You never made me feel pushed. But your encouragement did help me do the right thing in contacting my dad."

Nick looked down at his hands for a moment. They were resting on the table, big, capable hands that knew just how to touch her. She would miss those hands.

"He and I both agreed that we were idiots for going so long without talking to each other. You were right,

Becca. He never did blame me. In fact, all these years he's blamed himself. He's been carrying the burden around as long as I have, and we both agreed to set it down and move forward. We both missed so much."

"That's great, Nick. I really am happy for you. For both of you. I'm sorry I didn't get a chance to meet your father. When did he leave?"

"He's still here. He's taking a walking tour of Celebration. The woman who runs the inn set it up for him."

"Oh, you should be with him. Instead of here with me. This could've waited."

Nick raked his hand through his hair. It seemed like a nervous gesture, and it reminded Becca that she'd gotten carried away there for a moment. God, he did have that effect on her, didn't he?

"Actually, no, this couldn't wait."

"Oh."

Becca smoothed her skirt over her knees. If she'd known she was having lunch with him today, she would've worn something different. Not that there was anything wrong with her navy merino wool skirt. It was just a little plain. A no-nonsense outfit that had suited her mood this morning when she'd woken up. And, okay, it was one of the few pieces of clothing in her closet that she could still fit into.

No, if she'd known that today was the day she'd officially get dumped, she would've worn something a little more inspired. Something that made a man look twice—think twice before letting her go. But who was she trying to fool? This was who she was when no one was looking and she liked that person, even if he didn't. She sat up a little straighter, squared her shoulders.

There wasn't a thing in the world wrong with that version of Becca.

"Becca—"

Before he could get to the point, the server walked up to the table. "Hi, I'm Kathy. I'll be taking care of you today. May I tell you about some of our specials?"

She didn't wait for them to answer—really, it was a rhetorical question—and began rattling off the list from memory.

They quickly placed their order—a Reuben sandwich for him and a cup of clam chowder for her. She didn't have much of an appetite right now, but she was afraid that not ordering would've given off a hostile vibe. And there she was worrying about what he thought.

Forever the people pleaser.

No. No, she wasn't. She'd ordered the soup to make herself feel more comfortable. If she didn't feel like eating it, she wouldn't.

"So, what was it that was so important that you're letting it cut into your visit with your dad?"

He nodded and looked at her a little bit too long. Maybe he was weighing his words. Probably. Obviously, this wasn't easy for either of them.

"Two things, actually. I have something for you. But first, the thing that can't wait—Becca, I acted like a total jerk yesterday, and I'm sorry. You didn't deserve that. The accident wasn't your fault."

The old Becca would've told him it was okay. She would've immediately tried to set his mind to rest, but he *had* acted like a jerk, and it wasn't acceptable.

"I needed you, Nick, and you shut me out. I appreciate your apology, but whether or not we're together, we're going to be in each other's lives. We're going to have to communicate and get along for the sake of our kids. You can't just go inward and refuse to talk to me."

He reached out and covered her hand with his.

"I know. Believe me, I know. I came from a home where my parents' lack of communication and constant bickering shattered our lives. And I know it's been an issue with your family, too."

His hand was still on hers, and it was wreaking all kinds of havoc with her emotions. Since she was the one who had brought up the fact that they needed to communicate if they were going to have a healthy co-parenting relationship, she knew what she had to say.

She drew her hand away, trying not to imagine that he looked a little bothered by it.

"Nick, I have to be honest with you. I have feelings for you. I have since that night that we sat right here and… I guess I fell in love with you that night, but—"

"Becca—"

"No, Nick, let me finish."

His eyes held so much tenderness that she had to look away because her own eyes were starting to fill with tears.

She wasn't going to cry.

She wasn't.

She couldn't.

*Oh, God.* She was.

"Look, you can't do this—" she said, but her voice broke, and she couldn't get the rest of the words out.

All she had to say was that he couldn't keep doing

*this*—he couldn't keep touching her like this, and, for that matter, he really shouldn't look at her that way, either—but how could you set boundaries and parameters on the way someone looked at another person?

She hadn't really noticed, but maybe that was just his face. His gorgeous, perfect face. Maybe that was how he looked at everyone, and she'd simply misunderstood and read way too much into it.

Touching, on the other hand—now, that was a clear boundary.

She took a deep breath, gathering herself to lay down the no-touching law, when Nick suddenly stood up.

Where was he—

He was kneeling in front of her. And the tears were still rolling down her cheeks.

She just needed to get a hold of herself.

What the heck was he doing?

*Oh, God.* What was that? A Christmas ornament? Why was he kneeling in front of her with a Christmas ornament?

"Becca, I got you that ruby necklace you tried on in the jewelry store."

*Okay, but you're holding a Christmas ornament?*

Oh, wait, maybe he took the necklace back.

"I wanted to give it to you for Christmas. But somehow it just didn't feel *right*."

"You really don't have to tell me this, Nick. It's an expensive piece of jewelry. That saleswoman put us in an awkward position."

"Actually, I found something else I wanted to give you instead."

He held up the Christmas ornament.

Becca's heart sank. Not because of the gift—it was pretty. She couldn't see it very well because of how he was holding it, but it looked as if it had a scene of a town—maybe a Currier and Ives Christmas scene. It was probably lovely, but did he really have to give it to her this way? Everyone in the restaurant was looking at them.

Becca swiped at her tears.

"I know I've probably done more things wrong than I've done right," Nick said. "I mean, we haven't even finished decorating the tree."

"It's okay, really," Becca said.

"I've never been very good at relationships. But one thing that I have done right is to realize that I love you."

Becca blinked, and her heart lurched. Had she heard him right? Surely not.

"You are the best thing that's ever happened to me, Becca. Will you give me a chance? Will you please give *us* a chance?" He turned the ornament around. *Our First Christmas* was spelled out in ornate gold lettering.

Becca's mouth dropped open as realization settled over her.

Then she saw that there was something else—something small and shiny tied to the ornament with a red ribbon.

"Nothing in the world would make me happier than if you'd be my wife. You and the babies and I, we could be a family."

He looked as if he was holding his breath as he untied the ribbon that held the ring.

As the cymbal monkey started up in her chest, she hadn't realized that she'd been holding her breath, too.

"Yes!" she said breathlessly. "Yes, Nick, there's nothing that I'd rather do than be your wife."

As he slipped the traditional round diamond on her finger, it winked and glittered in the afternoon light streaming in through the large, leaded glass windows, and everyone at the tables around them broke into applause.

## *Epilogue*

On Christmas Eve, Becca's father walked her down the aisle of the Celebration Chapel. On her journey, she took a moment to look at everyone who had gathered for the happiest day of her life.

When her gaze landed on Nick, who was standing amid the red and white poinsettias that decorated the altar, smiling at her with so much love in his eyes, she knew without a doubt that she was the luckiest woman in the world.

And when the minister asked, "Who gives this woman in marriage?" her father said a resolute, "Her mother and I do."

The words made Becca's breath hitch.

Then her father lifted the blusher on her veil and planted a kiss on her cheek before placing her hand in Nick's.

Her sister, Rosanna, was her maid of honor. She looked stunning in her close-fitting red velvet dress. She gently took Becca's bouquet of red roses, while Kate, who was her bridesmaid, straightened the train of Becca's dress so that it lay perfectly, showing off the traditional line of the silk-and-lace ball-gown-style dress.

Since they'd planned the wedding in short order, Becca had allowed Rosanna and Kate to choose their own dresses. The only mandates Becca gave were the dresses had to complement each other, and they had to be in the same color family as the ruby necklace that Nick had given her. Becca was wearing it as her *something new*.

The wedding dress was her something old. It was her mother's. A seamstress had worked her magic to alter the dress to accommodate Becca's growing baby bump, and even if Becca had had years to plan and have a dress custom made, it would've been exactly like the shimmering lace-and-silk ball gown her mother had worn when she'd married Becca's father.

Isabel had a lot of quirks, but she also had impeccable, timeless taste.

Kate had lent her a pair of diamond earrings that were the perfect understated complement to the more ornate ruby necklace. And her something blue? It was her garter, hidden beneath the yards and yards of material that made up her voluminous skirt.

Nick's father was his best man. He'd been able to get additional time off from work, and he stood next to Nick looking handsome in a traditional black tux. Liam served as a groomsman.

Becca heard a sniffle in the front row and turned to see her mother brushing away a tear. Isabel had been remarkably cooperative over the past two weeks as they'd planned the wedding in warp speed. Her mother mouthed a silent *I love you*. Becca blew her a kiss, and with that, she turned to her husband-to-be.

As Nick reached out and took her hands, she looked into his dark brown eyes and saw her future: they would love each other for better or worse, richer or poorer; in good times and in bad.

They'd already been through so much and had found love on the other side. She couldn't wait to start their life together.

Her heart beat an anxious staccato, but it was a far cry from the frantic cymbal monkey who seemed to have gotten lost shortly after Nick had proposed. The eager excitement made her breath catch, and it was the best feeling Becca could imagine.

Nick was the love of her life. She had a feeling he would always give her butterflies. That's how much she loved this man.

Together, they would be a family.

*A family.*

The only place she wanted to be was in the arms of the handsome man standing in front of her.

She'd loved him from the moment she'd first set eyes on him. In fact, in some form or another, she'd been searching for him her entire life. Now she'd finally found him.

She knew, without a shadow of a doubt, that there was no place in the world that she would rather be than right here, proclaiming her love for him in front of God and the entire world. And when a single tear rolled out of the corner of Nick's eye as he said his vows, she knew that they both had found their happily-ever-after.

\* \* \* \* \*

## Available November 17, 2015

### #2443 A COLD CREEK CHRISTMAS STORY
*Cowboys of Cold Creek* • by RaeAnne Thayne

When librarian Celeste Nichols's children's book becomes a success, she's stunned. Enter Flynn Delaney, her childhood crush, and his young daughter, who could use some of Celeste's storytelling magic since her mother passed away. With the help of Cupid and Santa, this trio might just have the best Christmas yet!

### #2444 CARTER BRAVO'S CHRISTMAS BRIDE
*The Bravos of Justice Creek* • by Christine Rimmer

Carter Bravo wants to settle down...but he's not looking for love. So he asks his best friend, Paige Kettleman, to be his fiancée on a trial basis. What could go wrong? Neither Carter nor Paige can imagine that unexpected love is Santa's gift to them this year!

### #2445 MERRY CHRISTMAS, BABY MAVERICK!
*Montana Mavericks: What Happened at the Wedding?*
by Brenda Harlen

Rust Creek Falls' top secret gossip columnist, Kayla Dalton, has the inside scoop on her high school crush, Trey Strickland. The Thunder Canyon cowboy is going to be a daddy! How does she know? Because she's pregnant with his baby!

### #2446 A PRINCESS UNDER THE MISTLETOE
*Royal Babies* • by Leanne Banks

To protect herself, Princess Sasha Tarisse goes incognito as a nanny to handsome widower Gavin Sinclair's two young children. But what happens when the damsel-in-disguise and the dashing dad fall for one another under the mistletoe?

### #2447 CHRISTMAS ON THE SILVER HORN RANCH
*Men of the West* • by Stella Bagwell

Injured rancher Bowie Calhoun claims he doesn't need a nurse, but he changes his mind when he sees gorgeous Ava Archer. Despite the sparks flying, the beautiful widow tries to keep her distance from the reckless playboy: she wants a family, not a fling! But not even Ava can resist the pull of true love...

### #2448 HIGH COUNTRY CHRISTMAS
*The Brands of Montana* • by Joanna Sims

Cowboy Tyler Brand lives a carefree life—so he's shocked when his fling with London Davenport produces a baby-to-be. The Montana man is determined to do right by London, but she's got secrets aplenty to keep them apart. It'll take a Christmas miracle to get these two together forever!

---

# Turn your love of reading into rewards you'll love with
# Harlequin My Rewards

**Join for FREE today at
www.HarlequinMyRewards.com**

Earn **FREE BOOKS** of your choice.

Experience **EXCLUSIVE OFFERS** and contests.

Enjoy **BOOK RECOMMENDATIONS**
selected just for you.

**PLUS!** Sign up now
and get **500** points
right away!

Earn
**FREE**
REWARDS
Join
Today!
HarlequinMyRewards.com

MYR16R

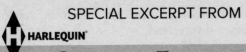
"Okay," Olivia said in a dejected voice. "Thank you for bringing me down here to meet Sparkle and play with the puppies."

"You are very welcome," Celeste said. "Any time you want to come back, we would love to have you. Sparkle would, too."

Olivia seemed heartened by that as she headed for the reindeer's stall one last time.

"Bye, Sparkle. Bye!"

The reindeer nodded his head two or three times as if he were bowing, which made the girl giggle.

Celeste led the way out of the barn. Another inch of snow had fallen during the short time they had been inside, and they walked in silence to where Flynn's SUV was parked in front of the house.

She wrapped her coat around herself while Flynn helped his daughter into the backseat. Once Olivia was settled, he closed the door and turned to Celeste.

"Please tell your family thank-you for inviting me to dinner. I enjoyed it very much."

"I will. Good night."

With a wave, he hopped into his SUV and backed out of the driveway.

She watched them for just a moment, snow settling on her hair and her cheeks while she tried to ignore that little ache in her heart.

She could do this. She was tougher than she sometimes gave herself credit. Yes, she might already care about Olivia and be right on the brink of falling hard for her father. That didn't mean she had to lean forward and leave solid ground.

She would simply have to keep herself centered, focused on her family and her friends, her work and her writing and the holidays. She would do her best to keep him at arm's length. It was the only smart choice if she wanted to emerge unscathed after this holiday season.

Soon they would be gone, and her life would return to the comfortable routine she had created for herself.

As she walked into the house, she tried not to think about how unappealing she suddenly found that idea.

*Don't miss*
*A COLD CREEK CHRISTMAS STORY by*
New York Times *bestselling author RaeAnne Thayne,*
*available December 2015 wherever*
*Harlequin® Special Edition books*
*and ebooks are sold.*

www.Harlequin.com

# REQUEST YOUR FREE BOOKS!
## 2 FREE NOVELS PLUS 2 FREE GIFTS!

### ⊕HARLEQUIN®

# SPECIAL ⊕EDITION
## Life, Love & Family